Tiger Time

Alaskan Tigers: Book One

Marissa Dobson

Published by Sunshine Press

Printed in the United States of America

ISBN-13: 978-0-9886684-0-9

DEDICATION

To my husband, Thomas who spent many hours listening to my ideas for the Alaskan Tigers series.

To my sister Jenifer who loves tigers as much as I do. She inspired me to write the Alaskan Tigers.

Contents

Chapter One

Tabitha Leigh staggered up the steps to her cramped studio apartment. A plain white envelope was taped to her door. The envelope piqued her interest, but not enough to truly care. She was just too tired and her body too sore. Licking her dry lips, she realized the fever of a hundred and one was taking its toll on her body. Her weak muscles barely carried her up the steps, a clear sign of his tired she felt.

Even with her mind wrapped in exhaustion and her aching body making her miserable, she couldn't sleep. Night after night, she lay in bed glaring at the ceiling. Deep inside she felt a desire to move, to start over somewhere new. When she thought about where she wanted to move to, the only place she could picture herself living was Alaska. Odd, since she hated the cold weather and snow more than anything else. Beside her bed hung a beautiful picture of Alaska with the aurora borealis lighting up the sky. It was the last thing she saw before going to sleep at night. Her coffee table was littered with travel brochures and Alaskan travel books.

She grabbed the envelope from her door, planning to toss it on the table to deal with later. The moment her hand wrapped around it, however, a weight lifted from her shoulders. *Insane.* In that instant, her plans changed. The steaming hot bath she longed for could wait a few minutes. Plopping down on the couch, she tore open the envelope. The stationary weighed heavy in her hands. It had a soft quality to it. As she unfolded the page, the manly scent of cologne hit her nose, rich and fragrant. *Not from the landlord then.*

Dear Tabitha,

I was a friend of your father's and I need to speak to you immediately.

Please meet me at Tony's Bar & Grill tomorrow night at seven o'clock.

It's important.

Sincerely,

Ty

With the note in her hand, a bunch of questions ran through her head. Had he really known her father? Maybe he could answer some of her questions about her parents and why she was left in the state's care. *Even if Ty answers some of my questions, I don't know him or what he really wants.*

Foster homes had made her cautious of others and made it hard to form any type of friendship with people. Too many people were out for themselves.

She wouldn't go. She wasn't much of a risk-taker, and this was too big of a risk. As she laid aside the letter and reluctantly went to take a bath, her brain told her she was doing the right thing. But her heart wanted answers.

* * *

Ty Reynolds had been in Pittsburgh, Pennsylvania for three days now, and no matter how hard he tried, he couldn't get in touch with Tabitha. She didn't have a phone number listed, which shouldn't surprise him. Most people were ditching landlines for cell phones. He'd stopped by her apartment three times already, but there was never anyone home.

What he had to say to Tabitha had to be done in person. He couldn't write it in a letter or tell her over the phone. He'd made the trip from Alaska to break the news to her gently.

With no answer at her apartment, he was glad he'd come prepared. He taped the letter he brought to her door and silently hoped she would meet him. Tomorrow would be the test. *If she doesn't show up tomorrow, I'll sit outside her door until she comes home.* Time was running out, and he had to see her.

* * *

Relaxing in blistering hot bath water with lavender bath salts and a touch of vanilla scented bubble bath normally eased the tension from her body. Tonight, though, she was on edge. The letter's contents kept running through her head.

Saying he was a friend of her dad's wasn't something that would make her want to meet him. She knew next to nothing about her parents. They could have been murderers for all she knew.

No, they weren't murderers. The caseworker had informed her that her parents had died in a car accident when she was a year old. Not that she remembered any of it. Thanks to a very nice police officer, she had a picture of her parents with her that was taken a month before they died.

The Polaroid was the only treasure she had from the family she was supposed to have as she moved from foster home to foster home. She sank deeper in the tub, remembering the day the police officer gave her the picture. It had become her most cherished item, even now kept next to her bed.

A year ago, everything changed. On her eighteenth birthday, she aged out of the system. Her caseworker, Bev, handed her five hundred dollars and told her to leave.

Tabitha dunked her head under the water as the memory of how exciting and scary that time had been came flooding back. On one hand, she wasn't tossed from home to home like some unwanted pet. But on the other hand, she didn't have anywhere to go, though the fleabag motel she ended up living in allowed her to save every dollar she could. The worst part was not being able to find a job. It was an endless cycle. No one would hire her without an address, and she couldn't get an apartment without a job.

She was getting desperate when a little mom-and-pop family restaurant hired her to clean tables and wash dishes. She didn't care what work she did as long as she did something to keep a roof over her head. The day after she was hired, she found a little, rundown apartment two blocks from work and thanks to Alice, her best friend and fellow foster child, she was able to rent it without a deposit. It wasn't much—only a studio—but it came furnished, and that's what mattered. The day she moved in, she had nothing but a suitcase full of clothes. She didn't need much, just a roof over her head and a place to lay her head.

The bubbles were gone and the water grew cold. Tabitha wasn't sure how long she was lost in her memories, but it was time to move on. Grabbing a towel off the rack, she wondered if she would ever find her place in the world. *What is my purpose? Why Alaska?*

Chapter Two

Tabitha woke when the sun shining through her curtains hit her eyes. The bedside clock showed it was just before six in the morning. Three hours of sleep—not much to the normal person, but she was grateful for any sleep at all. Maybe taking it easy would help her get over the flu or whatever she had. She wasn't sure how much longer she could go on in the condition she was in. She was constantly tired and her body ached all over. She struggled through the days, exhausted, but laid in bed unable to sleep.

Unlike most people, she wasn't a coffee drinker in the morning. She preferred a cold glass of iced tea to push away the fog of sleep. The bed was only ten steps from the refrigerator, not far to go. But she didn't make it before someone pounded on her door. Whoever was knocking would a put wrench in her plans for the day. It was too early to be a social call, and at this time of the morning, it must mean something awful had happened or was about to happen.

"Tabitha, are you in there? Please, I need your help. Open up." Her neighbor and best friend, Alice, called from the other side of the door.

Yanking it open, she was ready to be a grouch. She wasn't a morning person. "Alice, what's…?"

Alice fell into Tabitha's apartment and landed on the floor with a loud *thud.* Covered in blood, Alice had black and blue marks forming. Her short brown hair looked black from the blood matting it.

Tabitha stood back, appalled at the state Alice was in. *How could someone do this to another person?* Anger had her trembling as she examined Alice. She wanted to comfort her, but she couldn't see an unmarked spot where she could put her hands.

"I took your advice and told him I'm pregnant." Alice let out a pitiful sob before she could go on. "He beat the crap out of me and told me it couldn't be his. He doesn't have any children. None of his other girls got pregnant, so I must have cheated."

Tabitha listened to Alice ramble on as she grabbed her cell phone off the stand by the couch. The phone was the only luxury she could afford. It was an expensive thing to keep up, but walking home late at night by herself in Pittsburgh…she needed it just in case. Tabitha dialed 911, hoping an ambulance could get there in time to save Alice and the baby, and maybe the police could arrest the creep.

"911. What's your emergency?"

Tabitha wished there was something she could do for Alice, but the only thing she could give her was comfort. She knelt close to her neighbor, gently wrapping her arms around Alice. "My friend is in real bad shape. We need an ambulance. She's pregnant, and I think she might be having a miscarriage, and she was beaten badly."

"What's your location?"

"5050 East Liberty Street, apartment three on the second floor."

"Okay, I have an ambulance on its way. Can you tell me what happened?"

Alice moaned in pain. Tabitha spoke louder for the dispatcher to hear. "I don't know. She's my neighbor, and she came banging on my door. She told me her boyfriend beat her."

"I am sending the police out also."

Alice must have overheard because she whispered, "No, please. He'll kill me."

"Shh, it's okay. You're going to press charges and he'll be in jail, unable to do anything to you." Tabitha pushed Alice's hair off her face, holding her to her body.

The 911 dispatcher continued to gather information for her report, and Tabitha answered them but her mind was racing. *Could*

Mike have followed her to finish the job he started? Will he come back later looking for her?

Two paramedics rushed up the stairs, leaving no time to quiet Alice's fears.

Tabitha spoke into her cell phone again. "Thank you, the ambulance and fire department are here."

"You're in good hands now," the operator said before the line went dead.

Tabitha closed her phone and tried to step aside, allowing the paramedics room to assess her friend, but Alice grabbed Tabitha's shirt. "Please stay. Don't leave me."

The blond paramedic looked from Tabitha to Alice. "She's just going to move back a little so I can help you. She can go with you in the ambulance if you like."

Eyes wide, Alice looked like a scared child. "Please come with me. I don't want to be alone."

Tabitha brushed some hair off her friend's face. "Sure, I'll go. But let them look you over." After a slight hesitation, Alice nodded in agreement. While the paramedics examined her, Tabitha took the time to change out of her sweats and into a pair of jeans.

She'd just stepped out of the bathroom when the blond paramedic looked over his shoulder. "Miss, if you're going with us, we need to go. She's lost a lot of blood."

While they loaded Alice onto the stretcher and prepared to move her, Tabitha grabbed her purse and keys. She followed them down the steps and out to the waiting ambulance. As the ambulance pulled away from the curb, Alice passed out.

"Josh, call it in. The victim is out, and she's going to need blood when we get there." Then he turned to Tabitha. "Do you know her blood type and if she is on any medication?"

How could all of this be happening? Tabitha sat there in shock for what seemed like ages. The blond paramedic reached over and touched her arm. His question clarified in her mind, and she shook her head to clear it.

"No, I don't know her blood type, but she wasn't taking anything. Maybe prenatal vitamins. She was so happy she got pregnant and didn't want to do anything that might hurt the baby." She looked at her friend lying so still and death-like on the gurney, blood soaking her jeans. *The baby.*

Tabitha just looked at him, tears filling her eyes, and said, "She lost the baby?" It wasn't really a question. She already knew the answer.

He nodded. "I believe so. I'm sorry."

The rest of the trip was a blur.

* * *

Upon arriving at the hospital, she tried to stay out of the way. It wasn't too hard since Alice was still unconscious and didn't need her. She stood against the wall away from everyone. *How could that good-for-nothing jerk do this?* You didn't love someone if you beat them. That wasn't love.

Lost in her thoughts, she didn't even notice the blond paramedic come up to her with a police officer at his side. "Miss, Officer O'Malley would like to have a word with you, if that's all right?"

"Yes, but I don't know if I can be of any help."

"Thank you, Jason. If you will excuse us." The officer led her over to the chairs in the hallway. "What's your name?"

"Tabitha Leigh." She perched on the chair that allowed her a clear view into Alice's room.

When Officer O'Malley looked up from his notebook, his face was stone-cold and blank. A true cop's face. "Miss Leigh, what happened this morning?"

She tried not to cry as she thought back to how she got dragged into this and to the hospital. "When I woke up, Alice was pounding on my door begging me to help her. She told me her boyfriend did this."

"What is her boyfriend's name? Why would her boyfriend do this?"

"I don't know him. Alice refers to him only as Mike. He did this because she is pregnant. He told her he doesn't want children and since he doesn't want them, he believes he can't have them, so she must have cheated."

Without blinking, Officer O'Malley asked, "Is she sure this is his baby?"

She couldn't control the tears running down her face. It was unbelievable he had the nerve to ask that when her friend was in there dying. "She said it was. But I wasn't there. I don't know who she is sleeping with, but I have known her for years, and she is more honest and trustworthy than most people. She wouldn't tell him it was his child if she wasn't sure. She wouldn't cheat while she is in a committed relationship." Her voice rose with emotions. She wanted to be with her friend, not sitting here answering the officer's questions.

"We're going to have to question the boyfriend. Do you know where I might be able to find Mike?"

"No." With that, she was done with his interrogation. She stood and walked back to Alice's room. She wouldn't sit there listening to him. He was just like all of the other people in her life—foster parents who would never believe she didn't do something wrong, but she had taken all the blame. Well, Alice wasn't going to take the blame this time. There was nothing she could do to make him believe the story if he wanted to doubt it.

"Miss Leigh, I might need to ask you a few more questions later," her interrogator called after her.

Without turning to look at him, Tabitha replied, "You know where to find me, but I don't know what help I can be."

* * *

She didn't want to leave in case Alice woke up. The doctors said it could be a while. The day passed, and she stayed glued to the hospital bed waiting for her friend to come to. Darkness fell and her eyes were getting heavy when Alice finally woke.

"Thanks." Her voice was hoarse.

Tabitha poured a glass of ice water from the pitcher the nurse had brought in a little while ago and handed it to Alice. "There is no need for thanks. If you need anything, I'm here. I'll stay as long as you need me."

Alice tried to sit up to take a drink from the glass. She winced from the pain but managed to force her body into a reclined position. "I feel awful. Tell me what you know. Will the baby be all right?"

"I better get the doctor." Tabitha stood and walked toward the door.

"That bastard killed my baby, didn't he?" Alice screamed as tears started to flow down her cheeks.

Her heart broke for her friend. She wanted to do something to make things better. Give her the baby she'd lost, but there was nothing she could do. She went to her and held her close. Doctor Roberts rushed in.

Alice was crying so hard and was so upset that the doctor gave her a shot to help her sleep. As Alice closed her eyes, Tabitha laid her back down on the bed.

"I thought I gave you instructions to page a doctor and not to tell her that she lost the baby," Doctor Roberts said, standing at the side of the bed her eyebrows knitted together.

She whipped her head around so fast, she couldn't believe it was still attached to her body. "I didn't tell her anything. When I wouldn't answer her questions and I tried to get a doctor, she freaked out. There was nothing I could do. She just knew." Tabitha raised her hands in a "what can I do" gesture.

Doctor Roberts looked from her to the nurse. "Why is it that the family and friends always think they know what is best for the patient and disregard the doctors' orders?" With that, he stormed out of the room. *They're all the same. No one believes what I have to say.*

Tabitha sank down into the chair by Alice's bed and began to cry. The nice nurse who had brought the pitcher hung back after the doctor left and said, “Miss, she's going to sleep through the night. Why don't you go home and get a good night’s rest? She's in good hands. When you come back in the morning, she’ll be awake and will need you.”

“Maybe you’re right. Could I leave my number and if anything changes, you can give me a call?”

The nurse nodded and handed her a pen and paper.

She wrote her number on it and handed it back. As the nurse walked out, Tabitha leaned over the bed. “Alice, I’m going home to sleep. I’ll be back in the morning. You rest, and we’ll figure something out tomorrow.” She kissed her friend’s forehead before grabbing her purse to leave.

* * *

It was a nice, cool October evening. To save some money, she decided to walk home. It was only ten blocks. Pittsburgh was a beautiful city with lots of different shops and so many lights. If the crime rate wasn't so high, it would be the perfect city to live in. But as it was, a young woman walking on the streets at night alone had to worry about being mugged or raped. She kept her hand inside her coat where her cell phone and a can of pepper spray were kept in case she needed it.

The walk home gave her time to think about Alice and how things had turned out for her. Tabitha suspected Mike had hit Alice before, but of course Alice had denied it. Her friend wouldn't listen, and now look at her. *She could have died!* Tabitha's angry thoughts were close to the surface and threatening to overtake her. She didn't understand it, but lately, she was more emotional. Could it be because of the bug she had?

Chapter Three

Tabitha screamed and jumped up quickly when she felt the solid body against hers. "Who the hell are you?"

"Don't scream, Tabitha. You didn't meet me tonight. I wanted to make sure you were all right. When I arrived, there was blood in the hall, your door was open, and I came in. There was more blood in your apartment. I called the hospitals, and they had no listings under your name, so I stayed here to see if you would return."

While he spoke, she noticed his body. He must have been two hundred and twenty pounds, all of it muscle. He had arms the size of her waist. He reminded her of one of the biker guys who came into the restaurant. His chin-length black hair and broad shoulders gave him a menacing look. The only thing that hinted he might have a softer side was his spectacular, ocean blue eyes. His hair, brushing against the collar of his shirt, made her want to run her hands through it to see if it was as soft as it looked. But not right now.

"Back up. How do you know my name?"

"Didn't you get the note I left on your door yesterday? My name is Ty Reynolds. I was a friend of your father's." He sat there on the couch watching her, careful not to move as if worried he'd scare her.

Shock must have shown on her face, because before she could say anything, he added, "I'm not here to hurt you. If I wanted to hurt you, I would have done so already. I made a promise to your father that when you were old enough, I would tell you everything, and I would do everything I could to protect you."

My caseworker must have had the information wrong. If this man was a friend of dad's, then he had to be a murder or into some deep shit. At this moment in time, however, she didn't care. "I don't care who you are. I want you out of my apartment!" She walked over to her door and opened it. "Please leave."

"Listen, Tabitha, I know you're scared, but you need to listen to me. Please just give me ten minutes."

"You broke into my apartment and now you want me to listen to you? I don't want anything to do with you."

He made no attempt to even move toward the door. "Tabitha, I know you're not feeling like yourself. You're running a fever of one hundred and one that no matter what you take, it won't break. You can't sleep. Your body hurts and is sore. You feel your body doing things it hasn't before; you're faster; you can smell and see better. If you read that note...just holding the paper would have eased the symptoms. I can help you if you will just listen to me."

"How do you know all of this?"

"Because you're a shapeshifting tiger."

A what? Tabitha stared at him in disbelief for a moment, unable to believe what she heard. Her vision narrowed as black dots danced before her eyes before blackness consumed her and she passed out.

* * *

When Tabitha came to, she was on her sofa with a wet wash rag on her forehead. She couldn't believe how sweet and friendly the stranger was being. It wasn't something she expected from a man his size. He appeared more likely to throw a man across a bar than attend to a fainting woman.

She tried to scoot away from him but there was nowhere to go on the couch. He made the place feel small, he was so big. "I thought it might have been a nightmare."

"Sorry, it's not. I'm real, and everything I have told you is the truth." He handed her a glass of water as he talked.

"How do you know about my fever and my other symptoms?"

"All shifters have the same symptoms when they are going through the change. If you are among your clan, it would be less intense but still there."

"But this stuff is only in books and movies. It doesn't happen in real life." Tabitha took the glass with a shaky hand, struggling to steady it as she raised it to her parched lips.

He perched on the sofa next to her. The heat from his body warmed her even as the cool water slid down her throat.

He brushed a strand of her hair away from her face, leaving a trail of fire on her skin. "I know it's hard to believe. Trust me, I had a hard time believing it at first also. Your father is the one who helped me through it. I was a foster care child, just like you. If it wasn't for your father, I wouldn't have made it through. Tabitha, you're going to need my help. I don't want to scare you, but if you don't have the help of an elder during this time, the chance of your death is higher. I know you have no reason to trust me, but please, let me help you."

"Were my parents also tigers?" *Was that why my eyes change from their normal hazel color into a fiery orangish when I'm angry? Or why as a child I would purr in my sleep?* It was so bad that she was sent home from a sleepover when she was seven for scaring the other children.

"I don't believe your mother was. I never met her. I know your father was. All the gene needs is for one parent to be a shifter." He knelt beside her, covering the cloth with his hand and pressing the coolness firmly against her skin.

"You said you promised my father you would help me and protect me. Why would he make you promise that? You don't even know me." Her hands were still shaking as she set the glass aside.

"Your father was receiving death threats. He knew there was a possibility he wouldn't live until you were old enough. He asked me to take care of you if he wasn't."

Could this be real? She sat up fully, her heart racing, her palms sweaty. She might have forced him to leave if she wasn't interested in learning more of her parents. "Why would someone want to kill my father?"

"Your father was the leader of the tigers. Someone from another clan wanted to take over our group. Your father fought him and won, but the other clan wouldn't give up. They sent him death threats and before he could take care of the tiger behind the threats, he was killed."

"My parents were killed in a car crash." Tabitha's mind reeled with this new data.

"Tabitha, there is much you need to learn about the shifters, especially the tigers. Your parents didn't die in a car accident. A car accident might have killed your mother, but it wouldn't have killed your father. Your father was shot in the head with a silver bullet. They just made it look like a car accident. The police officer who investigated it wouldn't have been able to tell. It was a very gruesome scene."

"If what you say is true, wouldn't they have found the silver bullet?"

"They didn't do an autopsy. They closed the case as an accident."

The tears welled up in her eyes. *Why was everything I've been told a lie?* She'd grown up thinking her father had slid behind the wheel drunk, resulting in the accident. She'd always assumed it was his fault she was in foster care.

"But I've blamed him my whole life." She placed an unsteady hand over her mouth as though a part of her wanted to keep the truth inside. To speak it aloud carried a stinging shame.

Ty leaned forward and clasped her hands in his as he stared at her intently. "I know what your caseworker told you. I wanted to step in and tell you the truth, but you couldn't find out about everything until you were ready. I couldn't put the whole clan at risk. There are so few of us now."

As she cried harder, Ty pulled her close. "Tabitha, your father was a great man, and he wanted the best for you. I will tell you all about him if you want."

Between the tears, she nodded. "Yes, that would be great. I never knew anything about him. I have a picture, but that's it."

They sat in silence for a long time, Tabitha lost in her thoughts while Ty quietly gave her the time she needed. All of this was a shock for her...his revelations, his presence, the feelings he aroused within her.

Finally, she got the courage to ask, "What happens next?" Her heart skipped a beat as she pondered what his reply would be.

Chapter Four

"What happens next is up to you. I must return to Alaska soon. You can stay here and continue on with your life. I can find a local tiger to help you through your transition. Or you can return to Alaska with me."

Tabitha sat up straight. "I can go to Alaska with you?" She tried to keep the excitement out of her voice.

"If you want to. You know, most people wouldn't be so excited about relocating to Alaska and the cold weather." He sat next to her in the place where her legs just vacated.

"Well, I'm not most people. I have always wanted to go there. Something about it calls to me. I can't explain it."

"That's not surprising. You would have the desire to go where your clan is. Right now, our small clan is in Alaska, and not everyone is happy about that."

“Why Alaska, if the clan isn't happy?” She was interested in learning about the clan and her new life. She didn't know where to begin, but Ty had given her an opening, and she took it.

“I took over the clan five years ago. Once I did, I assessed the situation here in Pittsburgh and realized staying here would only to lead to more problems. At that time, there were a few tigers in Alaska that needed help organizing. My Lieutenant, Raja, and I talked and decided it was best to move there and form one clan.” Ty tossed the rag he used on her forehead into the kitchen sink with perfect accuracy. “We gave the other tigers a choice to stay in Pittsburgh and be prey to others since they would be without a clan or come to Alaska. All but two chose to come. The two who didn’t come to Alaska were a husband and wife pair, and they needed to stay close to the Pittsburgh area due to an ill human family member. We found them a home with the Columbus, Ohio clan, because of their special circumstances.”

Listening to him, Tabitha could hear the love in his voice. It was his family. Would going to Alaska give her the home and acceptance she longed for? Would they consider her part of their close-knit family? She tried to put her worries into words without sounding scared or childish. “Will the clan accept me? I’m an outsider.”

Ty put his arm around her and gently pulled her close. “Aww, Tabitha, they will accept you. You are part of us. Everyone will be glad to have you back as part of the family. Many of them wanted to get you out of the system and give you a home among us, but we were unsure if you would even go through the change. Children with one shifter parent have a seventy-five percent chance of shifting, whereas if both parents are shifters, the child will be too. Growing up, you would have been in danger, because if you didn't change, you would be put at risk. No one wanted to risk your life. Since no one beside the clan knew of your existence, we knew you would be safe even if that meant in the state's care."

What about Alice? How can I run off to Alaska with a man I don't even know and leave Alice hanging after what Mike did to her? "Ty, I'm sorry, but I won't be able to go with you." Before he could say a word, she was up and in the bathroom with the door locked. The tears ran down her face, and sorrow tightened her chest, making it hard to breathe.

"Tabitha, I don't know what I said to make you cry. Come out here and let's talk about this. If you don't want to go to Alaska, I understand, but there is still more you need to know before I can leave," Ty said from outside the bathroom door.

She tried to pull herself together enough to speak. Her throat constricted. "Please just leave me alone."

"Tabitha, I can't leave you alone. Now come out here. I will break this door down if I have to."

She refused to move; she didn't want him see her cry. She didn't want his pity. Life was cruel and there was nothing she could do about it.

"Tabitha, I don't know what I said to upset you so much. Sit down and talk to me. If after that you wish me to leave, I will."

Washing her face in the sink, she caught a glimpse of her reflection. Her eyes were bloodshot, and her face was flushed from crying. No matter how she felt, she knew she couldn't just leave him standing by the bathroom door. She did the only respectable thing: she opened the door and faced him. "There is nothing more to talk about. I can't go to Alaska."

"Only moments ago you were thrilled to know the clan was in Alaska. Why did you change your mind? Are you still worried the clan won't accept you?" Ty must have noticed she looked unsteady on her feet. He wrapped his arm around her body and led her to the couch.

"No. I just can't go." Looking down at her hands, she continued but in a softer voice, "I can't afford it. I can barely make ends meet now." It came out in more of a whisper than she expected. She was hopeful he heard her because she didn't think she could say it again.

"Tabitha, you don't need money. You just need to agree to it. The clan is ready to accept you and pay for your plane ticket back to Alaska with me. We're your family. When your father found me, I had nothing to my name—I was living on the streets. He helped me get a place to stay and everything I needed. I want to do the same for you. I want you to return to Alaska and stay with me."

Stunned that he would offer her this, she just stared at him. She couldn't understand why someone who didn't know her would want to help. All of her life, no one had wanted to help her with anything. She'd always had to deal with things on her own. If this guy wanted to help her because of what her dad had done for him, then he must be very altruistic.

When she didn't respond, he tried again. "Tabitha, are you still with me?"

She shook her head to try to lift the fog that settled in her brain. "I'm sorry, what?"

"I asked you, will you return to Alaska with me?"

I have nothing holding me here. Alice will do fine on her own. I've always wanted to go to Alaska and here's my chance. Maybe I can learn more of my parents.

"Yes. When do you want to leave?"

"As soon as you're ready. We'll be able to help you more in Alaska, being around people of your own kind will help make the transition smoother. It should elevate the soreness. You'll still fell tired because your body is working overtime, trying to adjust to the changes happening to allow your body to shift."

While Ty spoke of leaving right away, she remembered Alice. "What will I tell Alice? After all she has been through in the last twenty-four hours...and now I up and leave without much notice. We have been through so much together, and now I'm about to run off when she needs me the most."

Ty placed his hand over hers, giving them a small squeeze. "You can't tell her the truth. She wouldn't understand. We'll come up with something."

"I know. But I must see her before I leave. She's been my only friend for so long." Again, tears threatened to overtake her. *What's wrong with me?* She wasn't a crier. All of the years in foster care had taught her that she had to have a hard outer shell. You didn't cry in front of people. You waited to show weakness when you were alone. People took advantage of weaknesses.

"I understand. Let's rest. In the morning we can pack and then see your friend. If you don't mind, I'll spend the night on your couch. Since I might have seen me come in...it could put you in danger. Until you go through the change, you should stick close to me or someone in the clan. It's a dangerous time for you. There are those out there who hunt us, were-hunters, we call them."

She grabbed her sweats from the corner of the bed where she'd dropped them that morning and headed to the bathroom to change. "You can take the bed. I don't sleep much."

A few minutes later, when she stepped out from the bathroom, she noticed he hadn't moved. He picked the conversation up where they left off, "If you would allow, I can help you with that."

A snicker escaped her lips before she could stop it. "How would you manage that? I've been to the doctor's, and there is nothing they can give me to help me sleep. They can't even give me something for my fever. They say there's nothing wrong with me."

His gaze bore into her as he rose from the couch and walked over to her. "That's because they don't understand your body as a tiger. Anything they give you, your body would metabolize before it could help. I can help you by just being near you. Being close to another tiger will help your symptoms." Pulling gently on her hand, he continued, "Come lay on the bed with me."

Without hesitation, she let him lead her to the bed. If there was a possibility he could help, why not give it a try? She was tired and though his presence was bringing to mind other bedtime activities besides sleeping, she needed the rest.

Just having Ty's hand on hers made the stomach cramps recede a little, and the tightness of her body began to fade. "Lay down on your side facing the wall. I'm going to lay behind you with my body snuggled against yours."

She looked at him for a moment, wondering if this was some cheap trick to get her into bed...and would she mind? *It's plausible, right? His hand in mine did help.* Throwing caution to the wind, she climbed into bed just as he'd instructed.

As their bodies came together, she felt a shock of energy go through her limbs, causing her to jump and try to move away. Ty held her close. "Tabitha, it's all right. Relax. That sometimes happens with shapeshifters. Nothing to worry about. Sleep."

When he lay with his full body touching her, she finally felt normal, whole and safe. She wanted to hear more about her new life and her family, but her eyes wouldn't stay open. For the first time in weeks, she began to drift into a deep, peaceful sleep.

As she was falling asleep, Ty said, "You will soon understand what that jolt was. We are lifemates. You're mine. I will do whatever it takes to make you understand that and accept it."

* * *

Long after Tabitha was asleep, Ty held her close, breathing in her scent. He snuggled his head into her hair and whispered, "You're more than I could have hoped for. I'll protect you with my life."

For years he'd wondered when he would find his mate. He'd started to give up hope. The clan elders said when the right one came along, he would know it, and there was nothing he could do until the time came. Finally, after years of waiting and searching, he found her, his mate.

His tiger—never one for patience—was demanding he claim her. This wasn't something he could rush. Tabitha had enough to deal with without forcing her into mating when she wasn't ready.

Chapter Five

She awoke to her cell ringing. By the time she rolled over to get out of bed, Ty was already going for the phone. He handed it to her.

“Hello...yes, this is she.” Sitting on the edge of the bed, she realized the hospital calling her could only mean bad news. “I understand. I’ll be right over.” As she hung up, tears fell down her cheeks. Not bothering to hide them, she looked at Ty.

“Tabitha, what is it?” Ty pulled her up into his arms. He’d held her all night. He held her as she cried now. He held her as he waited for her to tell him what was wrong.

“It's Alice. He killed her. She’s dead. Mike must have got to her. Officer O’Malley is there and wishes to speak to me. I must go to the hospital.” Her voice distant and mechanical with shock.

“Get dressed and I’ll take you. My car is downstairs.”

Her body moved in a daze, nothing registering yet. Her only friend for so many years was murdered. *How does something like that happen, especially in a hospital?*

Ty being there didn't even cross her mind. She slipped out of her sweats and into a pair of blue jeans and a black turtleneck sweater before heading to the bathroom to wash her face and brush her hair. She wanted to get this over with. From the brief time she'd spent with Officer O'Malley, she knew he wouldn't get more pleasant waiting for her.

She was stunned by her reflection. The dark circles under her eyes were gone. Her face was bright and cheerful again. She walked out of the bathroom and found Ty standing by the end of the bed, grabbing a shirt from a bag she'd never noticed. As she walked out, he looked over his shoulder and stopped midway through putting his deep red dress shirt on.

"Tabitha, you look amazing."

Her cheeks heated in embarrassment. *No one ever told me I looked beautiful, let alone amazing.* "Thank you. I feel like a new person. It's amazing what a good night's sleep will do for you." Her throat closed as she realized while she slept, her best friend was being murdered. *I should have stayed with her.*

Ty finished buttoning his shirt. "The change is close for you, and once you go through it, you'll feel better than you ever have. I'll teach you everything you'll need to know." His words conveyed more than he was letting on.

Ty buttoned his shirt, and Tabitha fought an overwhelming urge to rush to his side, to feel his strong arms wrapped around her again. She felt safe with him. She couldn't take her eyes off the top two buttons of his shirt, which had been left undone so one could see a little of his chest—and an amazing chest it was. He didn't have an ounce of fat on him; every muscle was toned.

She shook her head and told herself to get her mind back on matters at hand. "Let's go get this over with. With Alice gone, I have nothing but packing to do before we leave. The sooner we can do this and pack, the sooner you can get back to your clan." Everywhere she looked she thought of Alice. *My whole life I've loved and lost people, maybe I'm meant to be alone? Or will going to Alaska change this?*

He took her hand, "It's *our* clan. When I spoke to Raja this morning...." She must have given him a questioning look, because he stopped to explain. "Raja is my Lieutenant, my second in command." She nodded, letting him know she understood and for him to continue. "Raja wanted me to tell you the clan is full of excitement that you have agreed to take your place among us. They are putting together a party of sorts to welcome you home."

People she didn't know were happy she was coming home. *I can't believe how much my life has changed in less than twenty-four hours. I lost*

Alice, and found people who consider me family. People that obviously care about me.

* * *

Tabitha walked up to the nurses' desk, and the nice nurse who'd been on duty when Tabitha had left the night before was still there. "I'm so sorry about your friend. I don't know how he managed to get in," the kind nurse said in a gentle tone.

Officer O'Malley came around the corner. "You finally had time to come down. You were called thirty minutes ago! Your friend was murdered, and you couldn't get down here any faster? What kind of friend are you?"

The nerve of him to speak to me like that. He didn't know what I was going through. He didn't just lose the only person that ever cared about him. Before she could say anything, Ty spoke up, "Hey there, officer, we came as fast as we could. She was asleep when you called. She just lost her friend. There is no need to take that tone with her. She came down here to answer your questions, not be scolded."

Officer O'Malley looked shocked that someone would stand up to him. He was obviously a man used to yelling to get what he wanted. "You're right. I'm sorry. I don't understand how he got in. The camera shows him just walking in past the nurses' desk. No one was paying attention. The cameras caught what happened, and I sent another officer to arrest him. I just have a few questions for you, if you could give me a few moments of your time."

"Yes, I want to do whatever I can to help. She was my best friend." She didn't care for Officer O'Malley and his attitude, but at least he seemed to care that Alice died.

"Good. Let's go into the staff break area. That's where we're set up right now." He led them down the hall and into a large room with couches and tables. One of the large round tables was already set up with recording devices, files and tablets. "Please have a seat there. Do you mind if I record this conversation?"

Shaking her head, Tabitha took a seat at the table. She maintained a firm grip on Ty's hand. She didn't care if the officer recorded it. She just wanted to help Alice and put this whole thing behind her. Now more than ever, she wanted out of Pittsburgh. She wanted away from all these painful memories, of the plans Alice and she had.

The officer sat at the table across from her and clicked on the tape recorder, stating the time, date and who was present before directing his attention to her. "Tabitha, what happened last night to cause the doctor to give Alice a sedative?"

"When Alice woke up last night, she wanted to know if the baby was all right. The doctor told me to page him and not to tell her anything. I tried to get a doctor, but she just started crying. She knew her baby was dead and that bastard did it. I went to her and held her. I hit the nurse call button and when the doctor finally came, she was hysterical. The only way to calm her was to give her something." The memory and the feelings it evoked in her caused her voice to waver slightly.

"What happened next?"

"Once the doctor gave her the shot and she was asleep, the nurse told me there was nothing I could do for her now. She would sleep through the night, and I should go home and rest. I gave the nurse my number in case things changed, and I went home."

Officer O'Malley reached into one of the files and pulled out a picture of a man with black hair, about thirty-five, with a teardrop tattoo in black ink under his eye. "Have you ever seen this man before?"

She was startled as she stared at the picture. "Yes, that's Mike. But last time I saw him, he didn't have the teardrop tattoo. The video shows him?"

"Yes. He is shown going into Alice's room and coming out covered in blood. He is also wanted for the murder of another pregnant girl."

She started to shake as if she was cold, and Ty put his arm around her, pulling her close. As Ty's strength and warmth penetrated her clothing, the tremors slowed before stopping all together. "She was my best friend. I want to see him pay for this." Anger replaced her grief and caused a stiffening in her spine.

Officer O'Malley nodded as he spoke. "With this evidence, I believe he will never see the light of day again. If we need you to testify at trial, where can I reach you?"

She looked to Ty, unsure what to tell the officer. Ty understood. "Tabitha is going to be joining me in Alaska. If you need to reach her, you can reach her at 2087 Snowman Lane, North Pole, Alaska. We will be leaving as soon as possible."

"That's a big move." Officer O'Malley glanced from Tabitha to Ty, then back at her.

She smiled politely. "Will there be anything else? I do have a lot to do before we can leave."

As she started to stand, he spoke again, "One last thing. Did Alice have any family?"

"No. But I am sure you know that. We were raised in the foster care system together."

From the look on his face, she gathered he'd done his research on them and knew darn well they were raised by the state. He was just being rude by asking. Rather than continue that line of questioning, he switched tactics. "Are you going to be making arrangements for her body to be buried?"

"I don't have the money to make arrangements for her. She wanted to be cremated. I'm sure the state will take care of that. It's the least they can do when they gave us so little growing up." With that, she took Ty's hand and walked out of the room. She'd had enough of Officer O'Malley's rudeness.

Chapter Six

Instead of going straight back to Tabitha's apartment from the hospital, they stopped by the restaurant she worked at. She wanted to break the news to Betty, her boss, that she wouldn't be returning to work.

She spotted Betty coming around the corner as the waiter went to put their order in. "Betty," she called from their table.

"Tabitha, I thought you were off today." Betty's brown hair slightly graying at the temples was pulled back in a tight bun that she wore when working in the kitchen. She had a patch of flour on her slacks, as she spent most of the time baking. It was her passion.

"I am. I was hoping you had a moment to talk."

Betty gazed back into the kitchen, where everything looked under control, before grabbing a chair and joining them.

"Betty, this is Ty Reynolds, an old friend of the family."

Betty eyed him cautiously.

"My parents were good friends with her family. It wasn't until recently that we were able to locate Tabitha. I have asked Tabitha to come home to Alaska with me. That's where my family and I live. She will be with people who love her."

Tabitha watched Ty and Betty. She would miss her boss. She'd been the mother she'd always wanted. *Would my mother have been like Betty?*

Betty was a sweet lady who had taken Tabitha under her wing, slowly bringing her out of the shell Tabitha had built around herself after being tossed around from foster home to foster home.

Betty beamed at her. "Tabitha, you will be missed, but I'm happy for you. You deserve to have people around you who love and care for you.

After an emotional goodbye, Betty handed Tabitha an envelope. Hugs were exchanged, and they promised if they were back in the area they would stop by the restaurant to see her. Then they left.

As Ty drove, Tabitha opened the envelope. Inside was her final paycheck with a nice bonus, along with a handwritten letter containing Betty's number and the words: *If you ever need anything, I'm only a phone call away.*

Tabitha's heart skipped a beat as she read the note.

* * *

Tabitha closed her apartment door, and the toll of the day hit her like a semi-truck. She tried to push the weariness away. She had to pack. She wasn't sure where she would have started, but Ty pulled her into his arms. With her head resting on his solid chest, breathing in his cologne, she let the tears she had been holding back fall.

"Oh, Tabitha. I'm sorry for the loss of your friend. I wish I could ease your pain," Ty soothed her as she cried.

Looking up to him was somewhat difficult with the way he was holding her and the fact that he was a good five inches taller than her. "Thank you. I just want to pack and get out of here. Mike knows where I live. He knows I can identify him. What if he comes after me? I want to get away from all of this."

He didn't release her from his hold. His body stiffened as he rested his head on top of hers. "I won't let him hurt you. I won't let anyone hurt you. Tabitha, before you pack, I want to talk to you. I don't know how to put this, but I feel you should know everything before we leave." He seemed at a loss for words as he let go of her and walked over to the couch.

She tried to remain calm, but her knees felt weak with worry. She took a seat as thoughts raced through her mind. *Did he change his mind? If so, why couldn't he have said so before I quit my job?*

"Remember the jolt you felt last night?" Without waiting for her to answer, he continued, "That's what you feel when you find your lifemate."

She started to laugh. There was no way that was real.

"Tabitha, I'm being serious. I know this is all new to you, but I want you to understand what that means. You're my mate. If you accept me, then it is my job to protect you, to please you. You will be my world."

She stared at him, too amazed to form words. There was a whole other world than the one she'd grown up in. It seemed unreal. "But...I want to marry and have children."

"Oh, Tabby," he said, pulling her into his embrace. "We can do all of that. But maybe we should take it slow. After all, you just found out you are a tiger shifter."

She relaxed in Ty's arms. Feeling his arms tight around her gave her a comfort she'd never felt before. Everything was sinking in, but instead of being concerned about being a tiger shifter, the death of Alice, or finding the man that was supposed to be her lifemate, the shock that was forefront in her mind was that he'd called her Tabby. "You called me Tabby. I've never had a nickname before."

For a brief moment, a hurt look crossed his face. Just as quickly as it had appeared, it was gone. He looked as though she'd stabbed him in the chest. "Do you not like it?"

"That's not it at all. I love it. I always believed nicknames mean you mattered."

"Tabby, you matter to me. I have watched over you since your parents died. You have always mattered to me, and you always will. You are my world. Come on, babe, you need to get some more sleep. You haven't been getting enough, and I know you're still tired. We'll pack when you get up." They hesitated, neither of them wanting the embrace to end, but sleep was the best.

Between the long day and the last few weeks of very little sleep, Ty was right; she was tired. She wanted to curl up in bed and cuddle next to him. "What about Mike? He could have someone come after me."

She crawled into bed, and Ty pulled the blanket up from the bottom of the mattress and covered her. "Tabby, you're my mate. I won't let anything happen to you. I'm going to make us flight reservations, and then I'll lie with you. Is leaving tomorrow fine with you?"

Tabitha nodded, snuggling deep in the blanket as she watched Ty move around her cramped apartment. Dodging the sofa, he moved into the kitchen, where a pad and pen lay on the counter. He tried to speak quietly as if trying not to disturb her, but she could still hear him making reservations for them to fly home to Alaska.

Home? I have a place I can finally call home, with people who care. No matter how many times she told herself that, she couldn't believe it.

Growing up in foster care, all she'd wanted was people who cared about her and a place to call home. Now she wasn't so sure. She'd been trained to be a loner, to not rely on anyone. Would that have to change now? Could she handle it?

She lay lost in her own thoughts as Ty finished making reservations. She opened her eyes to find him standing next to the bed.

"I thought you would be sleeping. You've had a difficult day."

"I missed you. Won't you lay with me?"

Without answering, he took off his dress shirt and crawled into bed next to her, cuddling his body close to hers. He felt warm, and their bodies fit side-by-side like they belonged together. Like two pieces of the same puzzle final joined. She couldn't get enough of his warmth and the feeling of belonging that she found in his embrace.

Ty slid his arm under her head. Her check rested on his bicep, and their gazes met. He rolled onto his side to face her. He reached for her cheek, drawing them together until their lips met.

His lips on hers made her body tingle. It felt as if electricity was all around them, waiting to explode. It didn't hurt, just provided a strange pins and needles feeling. She didn't let her mind talk her out of it. She wanted this. Her heart knew this was what she needed, no matter what her head was saying.

He was her mate.

Gently pulling back just a little, Ty looked at her. "Tabby, I'm sorry. I don't want to rush you. The tiger in me wants to claim you as my mate now. Tigers are not very patient." As he said that, a smile crept over her face.

"You're not rushing me. I want this. I love feeling our bodies together. You're like my other half, and I need you next to me." She didn't wait for him. Instead, she leaned back in to kiss him, craving his hands on her body.

Ty started sliding up her black turtleneck sweater, when there was pounding on the door and someone yelling, "If you don't open this door now, I will break it down."

Ty jumped off the bed and grabbed the duffle bag at the end of it. In a blink of an eye, there was a gun in his hand. She opened her mouth to ask him what was going on, but he put his finger to his lips, motioning her to remain quiet.

Quiet? Someone was screaming and pounding outside her door, and he wanted her to be quiet? He stepped back toward her, lowered his mouth to her ear and whispered, "This could get bloody. We should head down the fire exit. I don't want to put you in danger. I'll come back and deal with them once I get you out of here."

She nodded. She turned to grab the picture of her parents from the bedside table. If she didn't make it back to her apartment, she wanted to have the memento. Tossing it into her purse, she headed for the window. Ty already had his duffle bag slung across his chest, and he held his car keys out to her while motioning for her to go. She made no move to take the keys. "Not without you," she whispered.

Ty didn't take his attention from the door. "I'll be right behind you. You're my mate, I won't leave you. Now go."

As they ran down the fire escape, the sound of her apartment door slamming to the floor followed them. It slowed her for a moment. "No, Tabby, come on."

As they reached Ty's car, which was right by the steps, someone leaned out the window and yelled, "You can't protect her forever. We'll find you!"

Adrenaline coupled with fright caused all the blood to rush to her head. Her breath caught in her throat.

Ty said nothing, just got into the car and sped away. Once they were out of immediate danger and Ty was driving outside of the city, she turned in her seat. "Ty, who were those men? What did they want?" She placed a hand over her still rapidly beating heart.

He didn't take his eyes off the road. She wasn't sure if that was because of the speed they were traveling or because he couldn't look at her. "That was Pierce and his gang. Pierce is the were-tiger who killed your parents."

"What? You mean that's him? He looks to be only in his twenties."

Ty briefly looked away from the road and raised an eyebrow at her. "I tell you he's the one who killed your parents, and all you can think about is how old he looks? Most people would want to go back and kill him themself."

"Well, trust me, it's not like I wouldn't like to, but I don't think I could do much harm to him. After all, he killed my parents. I haven't even gone through the change yet, so I'm still basically human. But he looks young; he couldn't have been around when my father was alive." She shook her head in confusion.

He reached for her hand, bringing it to his lips. "I'm glad you have some common sense and you don't let your emotions get in the way. Pierce isn't as young as he looks. Shifters age a lot slower than humans. Pierce is really in his forties. Just so you know, the clan has been after Pierce since he killed your father. The clan has the right to demand Pierce's death for killing one of our kind. Pierce knows we want him dead for it, and he's been in hiding. I was on the original team sent to find him. We were on his trail for a while, only a day or two behind him, but he went into hiding. We have sent men out every time we get a hit, but this is the first real proof we've had that he is alive. I promise he'll pay for what he did to your father, but it was not worth it today. I couldn't put your life in danger to settle a debt."

"Ty, once I go through the change, I want to go after him."

He gave her a look that let her know he wasn't for that idea. "We'll see after the change is complete." His tone told her he would fight her on the subject later.

There was nothing she could do at that moment to change his mind, and it didn't really matter now. They had more important issues to deal with. She let it go and moved onto another subject. "How old are you?"

He left out a slight laugh before answering. "The better question is how old do you *think* I am? How old do I look?"

"Ty, don't play games. Just tell me." Tabitha crossed her arms and rolled her eyes.

He rubbed her hand. "Come on, babe. I want to know what you think. I promise to answer after you tell me how old you think I am."

"Okay fine." She looked him over, trying to guess the right age. He said tiger shifters looked younger, but she didn't want to guess too old. "Umm...Twenty-four?"

"So you're saying I look twenty-four, or that's how old you think I am?"

She turned even farther in her seat, rested her back on the car door, and propped her left leg on the seat, giving her a better view of him. Also, in turn, allowing him a clear view of the nasty look she was giving him. "I think you look younger than twenty-four, but you knew my father. I'm just now going through the change at nineteen. I would guess you went through the change when you were my age, which means you're a lot older than that, but if I guessed too high, it would be an insult. So please just tell me."

"Did anyone ever tell you you're cute when you're frustrated? Because you are." He grinned and briefly glanced back at the road. "I was one of the few people that went through the change at a very young age. Normally, the change happens in your early to mid-twenties. I went through it when I was nine. I believe the youngest person ever to go through the change and live was eight. That person was your father. I don't believe anyone has beat that record since. Therefore, I am twenty-eight. Does that bother you?"

Relief flooded her. "No, not at all. I was worried you would have said ninety or something." She settled back into the car seat. "Where are we going?" The yellow line in the middle of the road sped by, giving no indication of their whereabouts or destination.

"I thought it would be a good idea to get you out of here. I know this little place about an hour outside of the city. Once we are somewhere safe, I need to call Raja. I think it might be best for us to find a quiet place to stay until your change, before returning to Alaska."

She stared out the window as the guilt ate away at her. She didn't want to mess up Ty's life because people were after her. Plus, didn't the clan need their Alpha? "Ty, I would understand if you wanted someone else to stay with me until I go through the transition so you can go back to your clan. I'm sure you have someone you trust that can keep me safe. The clan needs their Alpha."

Ty pulled the car to the side of the road and after putting the vehicle in park, turned his body to face her. The look on his face wasn't friendly. "First of all, no one can keep you as safe as I can. I'm one of the best. Second, you're my mate, and it's my number one priority to keep you safe. The clan has Raja, and just because I'm not there in person at the moment doesn't mean they don't have their Alpha. I will be in direct contact with Raja at all times, and if I'm needed, we can be there in a matter of hours. The clan will understand."

Her heart skipped a beat. She'd never had someone care for her like he did, so much that they were willing to change their life for her. "I'm sorry. This is all new to me. I feel bad you're changing things in your life for me. I'm no one special."

"I know this is all new to you. Just let me care for you. You're someone special to me and the whole clan. Not only are you my mate, but you're Queen of the Tiger Clan. You are our Alpha female. After you have changed, you will take your rightful place beside me. They will respect you and love you the same as I do. Okay, maybe less than I do since I'm your mate. I don't want to hear you say you're no one special again." He leaned over the seat to kiss her. "You're going to be fine. I promise."

Chapter Seven

The rest of the car ride was quiet. Tabitha was lost in her thoughts, and Ty was giving her the time she needed to understand everything that had happened. Before long, she noticed they were driving in the middle of nowhere. On both sides of the car, all she saw were trees, trees and more trees. No houses as far as the eye could see. "Where are we going?"

"Not much farther. We're going to a cabin Raja owns up in Wind Ridge, Pennsylvania. Raja kept it because of the great location. It's right on the other side of Ryerson Station National Park, so when he changes, he has a lot of free area to run and not draw attention to himself. He loves to come back here whenever he gets a chance. He gave me a key before I left, in case I needed it."

"Why are they trying to kill me?" *Could Alice's murder tie into this too? There's no way. How could it?* She tried to shake the thoughts but they refused to go. They stayed in the back of her mind, nagging her.

Ty never flinched as if he were waiting for her to ask. "It's a long story, Tabby, but in short, your father's line of tigers have been given special gifts. No one knows why, but some say your father's line was among the first tigers, and you were royalty. You're the last tiger from any of the lines of royalty. You have to be protected at all cost." He rubbed his thumb over the back of her hands. "Without trying to be too insensitive, you must carry on the line. We are unsure what will happen if you don't. Some believe the tiger shifters will die off, never being able to have more children, and others believe that if you do not carry on the line, we will all drop dead with you. Most tigers will do anything to protect you. Pierce is not one of them. He wants to kill all tigers."

Thinking the whole tiger population depended on her was just too much to bear right then. She put it in the back of her mind to think on later. "You said he was a tiger shifter. If what you say is true, then why would he want to kill me? He would die if I die."

"Even if the tigers didn't die off with your death, he would be killed. I would not take it lightly that he killed my mate. Second, Pierce is not a born tiger like you and me. He was bitten. He cannot fully become a tiger. He can only change on the night of the full moon, and then he is a cross between a man and tiger. It is against everything we believe to bite a human; however, once in a while, we have a rogue shifter that will bite a human. That's what happened to Pierce."

“You said Pierce becomes a cross between a man and a tiger. What happens to us when we change?”

“You, my dear, will most likely be one of the rarest tigers alive. He looked at her with amazement in his eyes. “You father's line was Golden Tabby tigers, also known as the Strawberry tigers. Seeing your beautiful strawberry-blonde hair makes me think you will be a beautiful tiger. When you change, you will take the body of a tiger completely.”

Tabitha had never seen a tiger in real life, just pictures. It would be amazing to see what she looked like when she was a tiger. “You said I would be a Golden Tabby, but what do you look like? Are you also a Golden Tabby?” Trying to picture Ty as any type of tiger was hard; he was such a handsome man with black hair and bright blue eyes.

“No, I’m not a Tabby. I change into a Bengal tiger. I was a born tiger like you, so I change into the full tiger.”

She leaned back into the car seat, picturing Ty as a Bengal tiger. It made her wonder. “Can we only change during the full moon?”

“Since we are born-tigers, once we go through the change, we can change forms anytime. However, most less dominate shifters have to stay in their animal form for a number of hours before they can shift back and once they shift back, they sleep for ten to twelve hours.” Ty took his eyes away from the road to look at her. “You’re taking this very well. When your father told me what was going on, I freaked. I thought he was crazy and wanted nothing to do with him. I thought he'd escaped the loony bin."

Tabitha looked down at her hands, because she was scared to ask but wanted to know what it was like. "Ty, I hate to ask but . . ." She paused but figured it was worth a shot, "will you shift for me?"

Ty eyes budged slightly with shock. "I don't know, Tabby. If you get freaked out about what you see, it could scare you and make your shift harder. If you fight the change, it will hurt. You need to just go with it and let the tiger take over your body."

"But I need to see it. I need to know what's going to happen to my body. Will I still be me inside of a tiger body or will the tiger take over and make me uncontrollable? You're the only one I can ask. Please, Ty." She reached a hand out and laid it on his well-muscled arm.

As Tabitha waited for him to answer her, they pulled into what looked like a small, hidden side road. He sighed. "Okay. Please remember it might look scary, but really it's not as bad as it looks. Tomorrow night I will, okay?"

She leaned over to kiss his cheek. "Thank you. Just one question: how long until you think I will go through the change? Not before tomorrow night, I hope."

Turning his head slightly so he could meet her lips yet still keep an eye on the road, he kissed her back. "No, you won't go through the change before I can shift for you. You're close, but not that close."

Chapter Eight

The cabin finally came into sight after what seemed like a two-mile drive on the dirt road. "Once you're settled, I'll call Raja. If there's still cell service out here. I'm going to tell him to send a few of my best soldiers to protect you. They should be here tomorrow sometime. I'll have Raja get them on a plane first thing."

Slowly getting out of the car, Tabitha had to admit she was disappointed that he was calling in others to protect her. She enjoyed their time alone together and didn't want it to come to an end. She had hoped they could pick up what they started back at her apartment once they reached the cabin. *Are there other woman in the clan fighting for his attention? Will they be jealous because I'm his mate? Will they treat me different knowing I'm the Alpha's mate?*

"Tabby, what's wrong? Your mood changed once we arrived here. I know it's not perfect, but it's the safest place right now. Very few people know Raja has this." Ty opened the cabin door.

The cabin was small and cozy. A little kitchenette to the right of the door provided just the basics. The king-size bed with a red and black quilt was pushed up against the far wall with a trunk at the foot of the bed. Leaving the center of the room for the couch and chair. There wasn't a television, just a small CD player on the coffee table. Whoever came here wouldn't be spending much time indoors. *Maybe too small, if Ty is in a hurry to get away from me.* She eyed the bed and couch, not sure which one she could make it to. Her body was exhausted, and she felt downright awful.

She must have made the unconscious decision on the bed, because next thing she knew, she was plopping down on it. Her eyes feeling like lead, she wanted to lie down, but she could feel Ty's gaze on her.

Without opening her eyes, she knew he was in front of her. She could feel his presence the same way she could feel the sun on her skin.

"Come here; let me make you feel better."

"You should call Raja. He needs to know what's going on, and that way they can start making arrangements for your soldiers to be sent here." Her shoulders were slumped and her voice deflated.

"Oh, so that's why you're so upset?"

"I don't know what you're talking about." She tried to make her voice sound sincere and kept her eyes closed, knowing they would deceive her.

"You think I'm calling in soldiers so I can leave, don't you?"

"Well, isn't it?" She embraced her anger. Being angry was better than crying.

"Boy, Tabby, if you're going to be my Queen, you must learn how to read people better. No, that isn't why I would like guards for you. I want guards so I can concentrate on you. I don't want to run after someone who comes after you and leave you by yourself for someone else to harm. What if there was another attacker, waiting until I took off after the first one? I would feel better if I had a few more people close by, in case we need them."

Boy, did I read that one wrong. "Ty, I'm sorry I doubted you. I just thought you were trying to find a way out without being rude. No one has ever stuck around, so I figured why would you? Especially since people are now trying to kill me."

"Tabby, for this to work, I need you to trust me. I don't plan on going anywhere. If I need to go anywhere, I want you to go with me. That means if the clan needs me back in Alaska, then that's where you're going. Don't push me away. I'm not like everyone else. I'm your mate, and we will be together always. Once I have officially claimed you, you'll understand. The tiger in you won't have doubts about me leaving. We fit together."

Tabitha knew Ty was right, but she couldn't stop the human part of her from wondering if it was crazy. Her brain was screaming at her that there wasn't even a small possibility that she could really shift into a tiger, but her heart knew everything Ty told her was the truth. This was who she was and what she was meant to be, so she had to embrace it. She looked up at Ty and smiled. "I know you're right. I'm sorry. Please call Raja then lay with me."

Ty kissed her forehead before taking out his cell from his jeans pocket and stepping away from the bed. A moment later, the cabin was filled with his rich voice, making her heart pitter-patter. "There's been a small change in plans, Raja. Pierce attacked her apartment this evening."

A long pause while Ty listened to Raja. "Yes, we're currently at your cabin. I thought it was best to get her out of the city, and this was the first place I thought about. I need you to make arrangements for Leo, Thomas and Felix to get over to Pittsburgh as soon as possible." His shoulders rolling like he was anxious.

"Great. Get Felix here right away then. Have the other two fly into Pittsburgh. We'll pick them up at the airport when I exchange cars—with all of us we are going to need something much bigger—and then we can head there. Let me know when they're flying in."

There was another long pause, and Ty started pacing the small cabin. There wasn't much room for him to pass. He was a large man in a small space, which meant he only had to take a few steps in any direction to be at the other side. A low growl came from deep in Ty's throat. “Raja, keep me informed about the situation there. We can be back in a matter of hours.”

With that, he closed the phone and tossed it onto the bed. “Tabby, were you serious when you asked me to shift for you?”

“Yes. Have you changed your mind?”

“No, Tabby, I was going to shift for you now if you still want to see it. It’s a great way to relive stress and anger. Plus tomorrow, we’ll be driving, so I won't be able to.” Ty unbuttoned his shirt and tossed it on the back of the couch. “I won't do it if you’re not ready.”

Butterflies started to swarm in Tabitha’s stomach. His muscles were tense with anger, his hands balled into fists. Shifting would help him release whatever made him furious. “No, let’s do it. I need to see what happens. You won’t attack me or anything, will you?”

A mixture of a growl and laugh came from Ty's throat. “No, love, I won't hurt you. Once I change, I’ll still be me, just in a different form. A much bigger form. I have one request before I shift.”

She cocked her head to the side, waiting for his request. “What would you like?”

“I want one last kiss. If my shifting freaks you out, it might be my last kiss. Will you kiss me one last time, Tabby?”

Tabitha left the bed and eliminated the short distance between them. "Ty, you told me yourself this is natural and I'll have to go through it. Why would I be so freaked that I wouldn't want to be with you once you've shifted?" She stood on her tipsy toes, and not waiting for an answer, she wrapped her arms around his neck and kissed him. What she thought would have been a sweet peck on the lips turned into a hungry and demanding kiss.

Ty broke the kiss but still held her close. "Tabby, if I don't do this now, I will take you. As much as I want that, I want our first time to be gentle. If I take you in the mood I'm in right now, I won't be gentle."

Ty slipped out of his clothes and stood in front of the couch. Her breath caught in her throat as she stood in awe of his body. She wanted to run her hands over every inch of him.

"This is going to look painful, but I promise it's not as bad as you think. Just stay over there until I complete the change. I don't want to hurt you by accident."

Ty stood in front of the couch and started to shake ever so slightly. Slowly, the tiger fur started to come through his skin. The reddish-orange and black hair looked soft enough to run her hands through. Tabitha took a step forward, wanting to touch it, before remembering Ty's words. She stayed where she was, never taking her eyes off him.

The bones seemed to break and morph into different shapes, forcing him to fall forward toward the floor. Just when it appeared he would hit the floor, his body completed the transition. There in front of her was a tiger, and four large tiger paws supported his massive body. His mere size had her speechless. From head to tail, he had to be eight feet long and weighed over four hundred and fifty pounds.

He shook his body, fluffing his hair out, as he observed her. Tabitha watched, not moving from the bed until Ty lay on the floor softly purring. Taking that as a sign, she moved slowly, leaving the bed and gradually inching closer.

Even though she knew he wouldn't hurt her, she was a little hesitant about rushing up to him. Closing the space between them, she reached out to touch him before lowering herself to sit on the floor next to him.

Ty lifted his head from between his paws and laid it in her lap. She raised her hand and touched the top of his head. His fur was velvety. As she ran her palm over it, he let out a soft purr and when she rubbed behind his ears, his purring grew louder, as if he were enjoying the feeling. "Ty, I don't know if you can understand me, but you're picturesque. I have only seen tigers in photographs, but this is amazing."

Ty licked her cheek, as if to let her know he understood, and that's when she noticed his long, sharp teeth. Without thinking, she reached for them but then thought better of it. Ty must have understood she wanted to touch them because he opened his mouth and moved it closer to her hand. Inching her hand farther away, she closed her eyes, and she could have sworn she heard him say, "Go ahead, baby, touch them."

She froze in place. She would have bet her life she'd heard him, but she couldn't have, could she? "I must be crazy," she said more to herself than Ty.

"You heard me, didn't you?" The voice was in her head, not out loud.

Tabitha shook her head. "No, I'm losing my mind. This must be some kind of dream, and I'm going to wake up any moment."

"Tabby, it's not a dream. You can really hear me. I think we just found out what your power from your father's line is."

She wanted to turn this into something to be happy for, but she worried he might be able to hear everything she was thinking. "Does that mean you can hear my thoughts also?"

"No, you don't have to worry. I can't hear your thoughts now. I might be able to hear them when you're in tiger form if you project them to me. I don't have the gift to hear what others are thinking. But let me tell you that you're amazing. You have taken this all so well. Most people would have run off screaming by now. We normally don't shift for newbies."

She was still rubbing Ty's head. "You're pretty amazing yourself, big guy. I needed to see the change. I was starting to freak myself out about how bad it would be. It doesn't look nearly as bad as I thought it would. The only thing I can't get over is how much of *you* that you still are when you're in tiger form. I was thinking that the animal would take over more."

"You can feel the animal there, but it's not all consuming unless you allow it to be, and that's when we get rogue shifters. Want to feel the teeth? I know you wanted to earlier but thought I might bite your hand off. Come on, darling, I only nibble."

She had to chuckle at the last comment. "Only nibble, huh?" She could have sworn the tiger smiled at her. "I didn't think you would bite me. I just thought it wasn't such a good idea. They are so long and look so sharp."

"Come on, I know you want to."

He opened his mouth, and slowly, she started to move her hand toward it. He wouldn't hurt her. He was gentle and loving, but another tiger could turn in a moment. "They are so sharp."

When she moved her hand away from his mouth, Ty looked up at her. His crystal clear blue eyes gazed at her with so much trust. "Satisfied, love?" she heard him say in her head.

"With you changing, yes." She chose to keep silent about other things she wanted him to satisfy. She wanted Ty to claim her as his mate. "Do you have to stay like that all nigh—" Before she could finish the sentence, he changed back to human form. One moment he was a tiger and she was rubbing his head, and the next moment he was a naked man with his head resting in her lap.

"Oh my." She shivered from the magic in the air.

"Sorry, babe, didn't mean to frighten you. I was anxious to change back and continue what we started before I changed. That is if you're still in the mood?" He gave her a cocky grin, as if to say she wouldn't turn down a naked man in her lap. To wipe the smile off his face, she bent to kiss him.

Their lips met, and it was like a drug they couldn't get enough of. Ty leaned up, taking the kiss that started off sweet and innocent to a whole 'nother level. As their kisses grew deeper and longer, Ty slid her turtleneck up, parting their mouths only long enough to lift it over her head.

The sweater slid over her head to lie lost on the floor, and Ty kissed her neck before slowly working his way down to her breasts. He drew his tongue along the tops of her breasts where the cups of the bra hid the best part from view, as he slipped his hands around back to unhook her bra.

When the bra slid down to join her sweater, a purr filled the space between them, making her freeze.

"Did you just purr at my breast?" Her voice held the disbelief she felt.

He glanced up at her and nodded slightly. His mouth never left her breast. Taking her nipple into his mouth, he rolled his tongue around it before gently placing it between his teeth and pulling. Her thoughts skittered over those huge tiger teeth, but his gentle nipping stole her control. Her back arched, leaving Ty no choice but to loosen his teeth or cause her pain. He removed them from the nipple and slowly kissed his way across to the other one.

Ty pulled the blanket from the back of the couch and laid it behind her on the floor, and in a deep sexy drawl, he instructed her, "Lay down, Tabby, and let me pleasure you." She stretched out on the blanket, watching him with wanting eyes. He was the only thing she could see.

Ty leaned over her, claiming her lips before taking his sweet time kissing a path down her body, spending extra time for each breast. As he kissed her abdomen, his fingers worked to unbutton her jeans before he pulled them down her legs. Using her toes, she kicked off her sneakers, allowing her jeans to slide completely off. Once they were out of the way, his teeth latched onto her red thong, tugging on it until it broke free.

"What the hell?" she gasped as she propped herself up on her elbows.

"My patience wore thin." He cocked his head to the side, giving her a sly grin.

She had to agree with him there. He spent so much time and effort taking off her clothes, it was beginning to feel like torture. She'd never had anyone take her clothes off, and tonight all she wanted to do was be as naked as he was. She wanted every inch of their bare flesh touching.

She caressed his cheek, and he turned his head to kiss her wrist. Her face heated with awareness from the way he was staring down at her. "Let me make this time memorable for you. Mating is supposed to be special and all about the female. Lay back and enjoy this." She did as he asked, running her hands over his body, feeling the muscles on his skin contract as he moved and the warmth he gave off.

Look at him. I could never get tired of his body. His washboard abs that make me want to run my tongue over them and to have his arms wrapped around me as if I am his world. Now that would be the life.

She was jolted out of her thoughts by the heat of electricity sparking around their bodies. There was a beauty to it that whipped away any fears she might have had.

"Tabby, I need to ask, are you sure about this? Once I have claimed you as my mate, there is no going back. We'll be mated forever; we're not like humans. You won't be able to divorce me. If you have doubts, it's best to wait." His voice cracked.

Propping herself up on her elbow, she kissed him. "Ty, I'm sure. As you said, I'm your mate. Why would I want to fight it? I want you." She kissed him again but this time, she let her desire race through her. She wanted to chase his worries away.

As Ty entered her, she could feel the air explode around them, as if they had just unleashed something. He took his time allowing her core to adjust around him.

There was a gentle quality to Ty, not only during sex, which would have surprised many. Most would have just seen him as menacing and intimidating because of his size. She was lucky enough to see another side of him, a side she was sure not many got to see.

He made sure to please every inch of her. She loved his body touching hers. Every touch like the first touch. When she wasn't sure she could take any more and was at the edge of bliss, she heard Ty say, "Baby, come for me."

As their bodies relaxed, a burning sensation coursed through her right hand. A whimper escaped her, and Ty hissed as they brought their hands into view. There was a moon design burned into the tops of their hands.

Ty rolled off to lie beside her on the blanket.

Motioning toward their hands, she asked, "Did you know it would happen?" A faint trace of the pain she felt from her hand still in her voice.

"No, Tabby, I didn't..." He couldn't tear his gaze away from their hands as if he couldn't believe it. "Not really."

"What do you mean not really? Either you did or you didn't. Which is it?"

"Tabby, I'm sorry. I guess I knew there was a chance."

"You knew there was a chance of this and you didn't tell me?" This time she couldn't keep the pain from her voice. The searing pain from her hand made her testy, leaving him the unfortunate outlet for her discomfort. She was hurt that he'd tried to hide something like this from her.

"Let me explain." He must have taken her silence as a sign that she would listen, because he continued, "There hasn't been a tiger of your line to mate with another tiger in the last eighty-five years. There were rumors that it would happen if someone from your line mated with another tiger and not a human, but no one could be sure. It was just information that the elders passed down from generation to generation. I never believed it until now. I'm sorry I didn't tell you, but I honestly didn't think of it."

She could hear in his voice that he was telling the truth.

"So what does this mean?"

"If I remember the story right, it means we're the highest ranking tigers. Once you mated with me, it brought me into the line. It means we could claim our rightful title as King and Queen of all the tigers and not just of the Alaska tigers." He paused as if gathering his thoughts. "If this is a fact, then I would say everything that the book says is true."

Tabby could feel her eyes go big, and she wasn't sure she wanted to know but had to ask. "What book? What does it say?"

"Your father gave me a book to give to you once we were sure you were going to go through the change. No one can open it besides your line. But since I was entrusted with helping you through the change, your father opened it one evening and we read it together. If I remember correctly, it says there will be a female tiger that claims her place as Queen and unites the tigers."

"Where's this book now?"

"Babe, you are a genius." He leaded over to kiss her cheek before he shot up onto his feet and grabbed his discarded jeans. "I brought it with me. It's in my bag in the car."

Chapter Nine

By the time Ty returned from the car, Tabby was dressed again and digging around to see if there was anything in the cabinets to make coffee or tea. There was a slight chill in the cabin, causing her to shiver.

Ty must not have spotted her when he opened the cabin door because there was a slight edge of panic in his voice. "Tabby?"

"I'm over here. It's chilly in here." She closed the cabinet door.

Ty gave her a smug little grin. "Come here; I'll warm you up"

"Correct me if I'm wrong, but didn't we just do that?" Grabbing the book from his hands, she gave him a rewarding kiss.

"Honest, Tabby, I was just going to offer to have you sit on my lap while we looked at the book. You would be warm in a matter of moments. Once you go through the transition, your body temperature always runs at one hundred and one. But I do plan to do what you were thinking again later. Come on, we need to find out what is in store for us and if there are any more little surprises." Ty led her to the couch. Once there, he grabbed the blanket she'd thrown there from the floor and set it next to him. "On my lap and I promise to be good."

She *was* pretty chilly, and he was right; his body was like her own personal heating blanket. She sat on his lap, and he threw the blanket over them. The heat coming from him made her want to curl her body into him. He seemed to know what she was thinking and put his big arms around her, pulling her closer. She rested her head against his chest and opened the book.

There was a lock on the side of the book, but when she went to unlock it, it seemed to just spring apart.

"It did that for your father too," Ty said.

She turned to the first page, and there was a handwritten note addressed to her.

Tabitha,

If you're reading this letter, I didn't get to see you grow up, and I'm sorry for that. I'm sure you're an amazing woman. Hopefully you took after your mother more than you did me. But if you're able to open this book, you must be on the brink of going through the change. I always knew you would follow in my footsteps. I'm just sorry to see that I won't be there to help you through it. But I know you're in good hands. (Ty, you better take care of my baby.)

Tabitha, everything you read in this book is true and has been passed down through my family for generations. Now it goes to you. Everything you will need to know is in this book. I have faith that you will be able to accomplish much. I am honored that it is my daughter who is going to bring the tigers together.

In case you didn't guess, my gift was to know the future. I love you, Tabitha.

Love,

Your father

P.S. Ty, welcome to the family. Glad to have you as my son-in-law. If you were wondering, it's why I picked you. I wanted someone who cared as much about her as I do, even if you didn't know it at that time.

Tears were flowing down her face like a waterfall.

"Tabby, are you all right? You don't have to do this now."

She wiped the moisture away with the sleeve of her shirt. "Yes, I'm fine. He loved me."

He hugged her tighter to his body. "Yes, baby, he did, and he wanted the best for you."

* * *

They spent hours going over the book. It consisted of spells, names of enemies, important dates in shifter history and pretty much anything the elders of Tabitha's line thought might someday be useful to the tigress that would bring together all tigers. They wanted to pass on things they thought might be important.

When they got to what they believed was the end of the book, another hundred pages or so magically appeared. The first page read:

Tabitha and Ty have been chosen. Everything you read in the following pages has been sealed since the beginning of time. It will walk you through bringing tiger shifters from around the world together. Whenever you need advice or think you're missing something, come back to the book. It will know what you need and will show it to you. Your first step is to return to Alaska. The safest place for you right now is with your clan. Tabitha, you need to meet and get to know your clan. From the clan you will choose three other tiger shifters to help you on your journey. We have chosen a number of good tigers that you can select from. You will be able to tell them apart from the others by the gold aura around them. Besides the two of you, only Raja may know about any of this. Raja is your Lieutenant now and will remain once you unite the tigers. Once you are in Alaska and have decided who you want as part of the chosen team, you will be told what to do next.

"I guess I should call Raja and inform him there is no need to send Leo and Thomas. We will leave for Alaska tomorrow if that's all right with you. Getting you among your own kind before your transition will make things easier on you. I'll have Raja make us reservations, so we can rest."

She nodded in agreement, still shocked. *This is just too much. I went from being no one to someone pretty freaking special in such a short period.*

Before Ty could call Raja, his cell started ringing from the side of the couch. "Raja?" Ty answered his phone.

"About that...I was just about to call you. There has been a change in plans. I can't explain on the phone, but it's safer if we come back to Alaska. I'll explain everything when we get in." Ty still had his arm wrapped around Tabitha's back, holding her close.

"We'll wait for Felix and catch a flight out of Cincinnati, Ohio tomorrow night. Just to be safe, since we are flying home, I don't want to go back in to Pittsburgh. Will you arrange for us to have three tickets waiting at the airport?"

There was a short pause. "I will deal with him when I get home. Confine him to the one of the cells until I return. Thanks. We'll see you tomorrow night at the airport." With that, Ty hung up. "Everything is taken care of. However, I'm starving. You?"

"Surprisingly, yes."

"Raja says there's a nearby town where we can get something to eat. There has to be some stores there where we can pick you up a few things you might need over the next few days. We can get everything else in Alaska. Want to go? Or do you want me to have Felix pick us up some dinner?"

"Let's go. We should take the book with us. I don't want to leave it here, just in case." Tabitha went to grab her purse from the nightstand, and Ty placed the book back in his bag to put in the trunk.

Chapter Ten

"Dinner was delicious. Thank you."

Ty pointed the car toward the strip mall they'd passed on their way into town. "I'm glad you enjoyed it."

"I can't remember the last time something tasted so enchanting. I haven't been hungry the last few weeks, and when I ate, nothing has tasted right."

"I remember that part of the change. It was one of the worst things for me."

"But the raspberry cheesecake with chocolate sauce drizzled over the top..." She let out a moan as she remembered the taste in her mouth.

"I enjoyed watching you eat that. You savored every bite like it might be your last." He slid the car into a parking spot and turned off the engine.

"Gibs?"

"Raja said it should have everything we need." He grabbed the handle of door. "Come on."

When Ty grabbed a buggy, she gave him a questioning look. "You're going to need at least a few outfits to get you through until we're settled in Alaska. We also need a suitcase, unless you wish to carry everything in your arms."

"I don't need much."

"I can see you're worried about money again. Don't be."

I've always worried about money. Living paycheck-to-paycheck does that to a person. I want to make the money from Betty last until I find another job. I don't want to rely on the clan or the money my father left.

"Are you sure you can't read minds?"

"I think if I had that gift, I would know. You're just easy to read sometimes. Like I told you before, there is no need to worry about it. Everything your father had went to the pack, and now it's yours. Even if you didn't go through the change, there is a bank account set up in your name from him. You have everything you need. Your father's investments did very well, but why wouldn't they since he could see into the future? Let's get what you need. I would like to have you to myself for a little while longer if we can make it back before Felix gets there."

She looked at the vast selection of clothes in dismay. *No wonder I hate shopping. There is just too much to choose from.* For a moment, she almost wished she was back in her apartment.

"You better get warm things. Alaska isn't the wet cold you're used to, but it's still downright cold."

She grabbed a couple of sweaters and turtlenecks that she favored in the winter before moving over to the jeans.

"Tabby, just a suggestion, because I have heard women like to know what to dress for when packing. The clan knows their Queen will be arriving tomorrow, and they're planning a party for the next night. You might want something dressy to wear. I saw a beautiful dress around this display that you might like." He disappeared around the display, leaving her no choice but to follow.

"Why are they having a party so soon? Why not later, once I'm settled?"

"We should be thankful it's the next night and not tomorrow after we arrive. The clan is full of excitement to meet you. They just want to welcome their Queen home in style. This is our way. Raja explained the time difference and what has happened, moving the celebration to the next night. When we arrive home, you'll still have to come with me to greet our guards and high staff."

Ty held up the dress he'd mentioned. It was beautiful, a white sweetheart-cut dress, form-fitting to the waist, then billowing out to be free-flowing. It had a red and black belt design at the hips. As he turned it around, she realized it was backless. "What do you think?"

"It's beautiful. But isn't it a bit much?"

"Not for the welcome home party. Trust me, you need something like this." He tossed it in the buggy. "What else do you need?"

Crap, I going to need to get bras and underwear. It's crazy to be self-conscious about it when he just saw me naked. I guess it is either buy them or go without. I can't go without a bra.

She crossed the aisle to the intimate section to grab what she needed, while silently praying Ty wouldn't follow her. She grabbed the first few matching bra and panties sets she saw that weren't something a Grandma would wear. *If someone is going to see me naked, I want to look great.*

"You would look great in this." Ty held up a sexy, black, baby doll negligee with pink lace trim.

I always wanted someone who I was in sync with, someone who could finish my thoughts. Ty seems to be just that.

She could feel her cheeks heat with embarrassment. "You can't be serious?"

"Come on, babe, let's get it. I want to see you in it."

Alice always wore fancy lingerie, even when she slept alone, but I have never been one to wear that stuff.

"I don't know, Ty."

"Tabby, you'll look great in it I promise. Once you try it on, if you don't like it, you don't have to wear it. But give it a try for me, okay?"

"Okay."

Knowing she wasn't likely to wear the negligee often, she also tossed in a pair of red and black plaid pajama bottoms and a black tank top.

"Now you need a duffel bag or some type of suitcase for this. You know I always hated shopping before, but you're adorable when you're shopping," he said, leaning over the buggy to kiss her.

Maybe wearing lingerie isn't such a bad idea after all.

As they loaded the car with their purchases, she came to the realization she had more than enough stuff to last her a week. Ty insisted she get everything she would need, reminding her of the party. She'd ended up buying more makeup and hair products than she even owned in her apartment. Not a wearer of much makeup, she hadn't known what to buy. Ty's solution was to buy one of anything that caught her eye.

"Now maybe we can go back to the cabin. I have a few ideas about how we can spend the time before Felix gets in," Ty said as he pushed the trunk lid closed.

I wish we could meet Felix tomorrow. I want Ty all to myself.

* * *

They arrived back at the cabin to find another car already in the driveway.

"Shit!" Ty hit the steering wheel to emphasize he wasn't too happy Felix was there. "Do you think we could send him into town for something or to a hotel room?"

She placed her hand on his leg, rubbing small circles. "I'm sure there is a lot of together time in our future. Remember what the book said? I must meet the members of the clan."

She heard Ty leave out a soft purr as she continued massaging his thigh. "I know. But I wanted you all to myself. Am I selfish?"

"From what I hear, no. Even so, it's all right, because I want you all to myself too."

Ty pulled to a stop behind the car as they watched Felix step out of his vehicle.

"Ty..." Tabitha said, nodding to the gold aura around Felix.

"I see it, but remember they can't, so don't act strangely. We can't let anyone know about any of this yet. You have to decide for yourself if Felix should be one we choose. After you get to know him, we'll discuss how I feel about him and what I know about it. You need to make your own judgments about him first." Ty opened his door and was around to her side before she could grab the handle on her own.

"Thank you." She stepped out of the car as Felix joined them.

Felix dropped to his knees in front of them and reached for Tabitha's hand. "My Queen, welcome home. The name is Felix, and I am at your service now and always."

What? He makes it sound as if I'm the Queen of England. She shot Ty a quick glance for help.

"Felix, we didn't expect you to arrive this soon. I have yet to go over this with her. I'll have to walk her through it." Without missing a beat, Ty gained control of the situation, and the awkwardness fell away. "Tabitha, he's offering you his neck. When greeting a lesser shifter, you're supposed to bend and sniff his neck. This is an act to let the Alpha know the lesser shifter is subservient to you."

Feeling a little odd over the whole situation, Tabitha bent and sniffed Felix's neck. When she was close enough to breathe in his scent, she smelled dried leaves, pine trees and damp ground. It was strong enough to almost convince her she was there. A rush of pleasure coursed through her body. There was no longer pain and soreness in every joint.

Tabitha felt Ty's hand on her arm as if he were grounding her.

"Tabitha, you smell the clan. Everyone from our clan will smell the same. Other clans will have other smells. If you mean Felix no harm, then you kiss his neck. If you find him a threat and wish him harm, then you would bite his neck, at least until you drew blood, depending on the situation and the punishment you see fit."

She had no reason to harm the tiger shifter, and he was one of the chosen ones the book mentioned. She leaned in, allowing her lips to touch his neck, and placed a soft kiss there.

"You have now accepted Felix as subservient to you. This is how the pack greets the elders when they have been away for a while or they are coming for judgment over a crime. Felix, you may rise and sweep the cabin and grounds. Tabby, once he checks the cabin, go in. There is no use in you standing in the cold. I'll bring in the bags and then start a fire.

Ty grab the last bag from the trunk as Felix came around the side of the house.

"All's clear."

Ty nodded as Felix reached up to close the trunk. "Thank you for coming so quickly. I'm sorry to tear you away from your family."

"It's fine. I'm glad I was close. We need to do everything we can to protect our Queen from Pierce. She is your mate, the Queen of the Alaska Tigers. I will protect her with my life." Felix paused a second, as if he wasn't sure if he wanted to ask, "You believe the legends, don't you? She's the one who will unite all tigers, isn't she? If you believe that, you must believe if she dies, our line dies also."

Ty decided to confide in the man who had been a trusted guard for years. "I don't just believe. I know. The last meeting I had with her father, he told me it was true. That's why it was so important I watch over her and help her with the transition. If she dies before she can bring another tiger into this world, all tigers will cease to exist."

Felix looked at the cabin with sadness in his eyes. "Does she know?"

"I told her that's what everyone believes, but no, I haven't told her I know. She has enough pressure on her right now. I don't want the change to be any more stressful for her. She will make it; her father said as much in his letter to her. You knew her father, so you know about his gift."

Chapter Eleven

The men already had a nice fire going, and it was beginning to warm up the cabin, when Tabitha carried a tray with three cups of hot cocoa over to the couch. She'd always had a soft spot for cocoa on a cold night, especially when it was snowing.

She had the impression the men had known each other for years and were old friends. First impressions tell a lot about a person, and she liked Felix.

"Felix, if you don't mind me asking, what were you doing that you were so close when Ty called?" She snuggled against Ty's warm body and felt him go tense. A look of fear crossed Felix's face.

"I didn't think to tell her. Tabby, leave it be," Ty said.

She understood whatever it was, Felix didn't want to talk about it, but she needed to know before she could make a decision about him as one of their chosen team members or not. She would have to talk to Ty about this when they were alone. But for now, she didn't want to put Felix on the spot. After all, they'd just met. "I'm sorry—it's personal. Just forget it."

"No, you have every reason to know. It's just not something I like to talk about." Felix set his mug on the coffee table.

"I understand. There is a lot from my past I keep private. So just forget I asked and tell me about the adventure you and Ty took. I love hearing things about him," she said with a smile.

"My Queen, I shall tell you..." Felix paused a moment as if trying to gather his courage. "I have a twin brother, Henry. Growing up, the whole family thought we would both shift. Both of us had all the symptoms: the fever, body aches and pains, stomach cramps, everything. The time came to shift. I shifted. My brother's body wanted to shift; he could feel the tiger clawing at the inside of his body, but the shift wouldn't happen. We tried taking him in to doctors of our kind, but no one could find a reason for it. The agony was just too much for him. He went through a number of treatments to try to bring the tiger out. Nothing worked. He let the tiger take him over. The vibrant twin I grew up with is no longer there. He is, for all purposes, insane. He tries to fight anyone that gets close and has to be heavily drugged. Even though he is not in tiger form, he is still deadly. He has the strength and speed of a tiger. The Ohio clan has a doctor who works with mentally ill patients. He has been looking after my brother for some time. My brother isn't allowed to live among the clan and be treated by the clan's doctor. I tried to bring him among our clan, but we don't have the necessary means to take care of him. I try to get back and visit him as much as I can. Most times, he doesn't know who I am, but he is the only family I have left."

Felix spit it out as if it was a bad drink, and he was trying to get it off his chest. Tabitha could see the pain in him at having to say it aloud, but she was relieved to know. Leaning forward, she took his large hand in hers.

"Felix, I'm sorry. I didn't mean to cause you any discomfort. This must be difficult for you. After my change, please take as much time as you need to be with your brother. I'm sorry we interrupted your visit with him."

"My Queen, you are most generous. Thank you."

Mentally she placed Felix on the short list of guards to choose from. *He has the compassion and commitment that's needed. Instead of being with his brother, enjoying his vacation, he rushed to our call. Tonight he proved himself to me.*

Chapter Twelve

"With three hours ahead of us, I think you should answer any questions I have. I don't want any more speed bumps like last night," Tabitha said as Ty pulled out on the main road. Felix was following them to Columbus, Ohio in his rental car, and then they would continue to the Cincinnati airport together. There, they would catch their red-eye flight to Fairbanks.

"Sounds fair enough."

I have a feeling he will later regret this decision.

"Let's start with easy questions. What's your favorite color?"

"Deep red. Especially the red in the sun as it's setting."

"Do you have any siblings?"

"No. I don't believe I do. Like you, I was a foster child. My mother, who was a tiger shifter, was killed by a were-hunter shortly after I was born."

She understood how the foster system worked and personally didn't have a good experience with it. "Did you have a foster family, or were you in a group foster home?"

"Until the age of nine, I was in a group home. I was a problem child, always acting out. My caseworker couldn't find a home to place me in. No one wanted to deal with a problem child. Shortly after my ninth birthday, I got fed up with the system and took off. When your father found me, I had been living on the streets for three weeks. He got me a place to stay among the other tigers and helped me through my change. After my change, he got me a job with one of the other tigers who owned a little market, and there was an apartment above the store that I could live in. He had an elderly lady who used to be a high school English teacher tutor me twice a week so I could graduate. Without that, I never would have finished school. I couldn't attend regular classes because I still had problems controlling my shifts. It's why most shifter children attend special schools or are homeschooled."

"Will I be dangerous once I shift?"

He laid his hand over hers resting on his leg and gave a little squeeze. "No, love, you won't be dangerous. You'll be fine. When you first go through the shift, you're likely to shift to animal without meaning to when you're upset. Your emotions play a huge part in shifting. When you're young and go through it, your body is still changing."

"I don't want to change and get stuck like that for hours." She heard her own fear in her voice.

"Tabby, you're Queen of the Tigers; you'll be able to change at will. If you shift because of emotions, once you calm down, you'll be able to shift back. I promise I'll teach you everything you need to know. Don't worry." Ty brought her hand to his lips, placing a gentle kiss on it. "You'll be fine."

There is something comforting about having someone believe in you so much. When he says it will be fine, I believe him, and my doubts fall away.

A smile formed on her face as she realized for the first time she had someone who cared about her and would always be there for her. "You always make me feel better. Thank you."

The time flew by as Tabitha continued to question Ty. No matter what the question was, Ty kept his end of the deal and answered. With some questions, she really put him on the spot.

"Last night I noticed you have a scar from your ribcage to your belly button. What is that from?"

Unconsciously, Ty moved his hand away from hers and rubbed the scar as if it hurt. "Before we left Pittsburgh, some men from Pierce's gang found our location and attacked. I believe they were trying to scare us into leaving Pierce alone. There were only a few there when the attack happened, and I was protecting Tora, Raja's sister, who was pregnant at the time. Pierce attacked with a large dagger while I was fighting off one of his gang members, and he got me there."

"And Tora…"

"Tora survived. Her daughter is a little over a year old."

"Have you ever killed someone?"

Ty took his eyes off the road for a second to look at her. "Yes, but only either to protect myself or someone else. It's not something I take lightly or wish to do, but it is my job as Alpha. I must determine the punishments for tigers that disobey the rules. I, or someone I dictate it to, must hunt down and kill any rogue tigers from our clan. This is something we will have to do once you take over as Queen of all Tigers also. I have never hurt or killed someone who didn't deserve it. Are you okay with this?"

"I understand this is something that happens. But as long as you're not killing innocents, that's fine. We're tigers. I accept that. Which means things are different for us than normal people."

This should bother me, shouldn't it? But it doesn't. I understand this has to happen. Eye for an eye kind of thing, I guess. Funny until now I didn't realize I supported the death penalty. Will Mike get the death penalty for murdering Alice? I hope so.

"I'm still amazed you have taken all of this so well. Your father would have been pleased."

The rest of the trip to Columbus passed quickly. Tabitha was able to find out a lot about the clan. At only thirty-seven members, not including Raja, Ty or herself, it was like a large family . . . and it was now hers.

Chapter Thirteen

It was just before nine o'clock in the evening when they arrived at the clan's complex ten miles outside of North Pole, Alaska. Ty resided in a wing in the main compound, allowing him to be available but still have some privacy.

Tabitha took in her new home while Ty dismissed Felix by explaining they were tired from the long journey and time change. But there were things they would need to discuss with Raja before they could turn in.

Once the guards exited, leaving Raja, Ty and Tabitha alone in Ty's quarters, Raja dropped to his knee. "My Queen, it is a pleasure to serve you. I'm so glad you're among us again. You have been missed."

Tabitha remembered Ty telling her they would greet her like this since she had been away for a while. This time, as she bent to kiss Raja's neck, she expected the forest smell.

Raja rose, turning to leave.

"Raja, there is much to discuss," Ty said.

"Yes, My King. I assumed you would like to be alone." He stopped halfway to the door.

"That's true, but we must deal with the business first. There will be plenty of time after. Tabby, it's up to you if you wish to lie down or join us. I know you must be tired, and you didn't sleep long on the plane." Ty came to stand next to her, draping his arm across her shoulders, drawing her into his body.

"No. I'll stay. If I'm to be Queen, then I must deal with this business as well."

He laid a kiss on her cheek before leading her toward the kitchen table. "Come, Raja tell us about Hunter."

"As you know, Hunter isn't a new shifter and knows the rules. My understanding is he was arguing with his girlfriend. Instead of controlling his anger, he shifted in front of her. She was unaware she was dating a shifter, and most likely for good reason, because she freaked out. When she ran, he chased her." Raja paused, looking from Ty to Tabitha before continuing. "She was killed."

"Witnesses?" Ty asked

"None."

“Hunter has been confined to the compound since we spoke?”

“Yes. He has been confined in one of our cells below. He is very agitated.”

“Tomorrow afternoon we will have a clan meeting to announce his punishment. He’ll be unable to change for six months and will have no contact with humans for an additional five years. I’ll place the collar around his neck at the meeting,” Ty said.

“I’ll inform the members of the meeting. Tomorrow night is also Tabitha's welcome home party unless you wish us to move it to another night.”

Tabitha didn't wait for Ty to answer. “No, that's fine, Raja. I’m sure the clan meeting can be held earlier in the day. I look forward to meeting everyone. I have never had a party thrown for me. It's an honor.”

Raja nodded. “I know you have had a long trip and must be tired. If that’s all, I’ll leave you to rest.”

“Raja, there is more we need to discuss.” Ty went to retrieve his duffle bag from the entryway where they’d left their stuff when they had arrived. Returning, he handed the book to Tabitha. “Tabitha's father asked me to protect this book and hand it over to Tabitha when we were sure she was going to go through the change. The legends you have heard about her line are true. She’s the last of the first line of tigers. If she is killed before she can continue the line, the tiger shifters will die with her."

Raja looked stunned. "I thought those were all legends."

"Even after her father told me, that's what I thought too, until I saw the book come alive in her hands." Ty nodded toward her.

Her eyes widened. *Heir?* "You didn't mention the legend said I must have an heir or the tiger shifters will die. Why?"

"I felt you had enough on your plate. Getting you home was our top priority."

Tabitha leaned forward, setting the book on the table, before touching the lock. As her fingers came in contact with the metal, it sprang open and flipped right to where the book started writing for them last time. The words that had come alive for them were still there. If she was in Raja's position, she would have wanted proof. She turned the book toward him, allowing him to read it for himself.

"Let's say for just one moment that I believe all of this, and it's not some joke. Why are you showing it to me?" Raja looked from one to the other, a dubious expression on his face, as though he'd just read that aliens existed.

"We're showing you this because we need you on board. If you can't be of help, then we need to know now. There's a lot that will have to change if I'm going to unite the tiger shifters. I need to make sure I have a strong group of supporters and people who want the same thing," Tabitha said, realizing she wanted Raja on her side.

"I'm sorry, my Queen. This is all just a shock. What can I do to help?"

"Nothing at the moment. I need to get to know the members of the clan. I need to know who is part of the chosen tigers, then I can make my choices. Once I have gotten to know them better, hopefully in the next week or so, we can sit down and discuss them. I want to know Ty's and your opinions on these people, since you have known them longer than I have. However, the final decision will be mine and Ty's. We just needed you to know."

"I understand, my Queen. Thank you for including me in this. Is that all, then?"

"That will be all for tonight. We need to get some rest. We'll discuss this again soon." Ty rose from the table.

"Okay. Welcome home again." Raja bowed before he left.

When the door was closed behind Raja, Ty grabbed the book from the coffee table and said, "Tabby, let's go to bed." His tone made it clear sleep was the last thing on his mind.

He didn't need to ask her twice.

Chapter Fourteen

The sun had been spilling through the curtains for hours, but Tabitha and Ty were still in bed, enjoying their time together. Tabitha's head rested in the crook of Ty's shoulder while he rubbed his hand up and down her arm in lazy circles.

At the bedroom door, there was a gentle knock.

"Come in," Ty said, not bothering to get up. There were locks on the door to his compound, but he never bothered to lock them. The only ones who would dare enter the area were the guards.

"I'm sorry to disturb you, but the meeting is arranged for noon." Raja carried a tray full of food.

"Thank you, Raja. Please leave us to eat and get ready. Arrive back here promptly at eleven forty-five." Ty sat up in bed and took the tray from Raja.

With a nod, Raja was gone.

The food had Tabitha's mouth watering. Waffles were one of her favorite foods.

"We have some of the best chefs here. You'd be hard-pressed to find anything as good as they make. Dig in." Ty laid the tray on her legs.

The first bite had her forgetting how to breathe. The waffles melted in her mouth, and the syrup was sweet yet bold and full of maple flavor. Gaining control of herself, she remembered what she wanted to ask Ty before being sidetracked by the aroma. "Why did you ask Raja to join us before the clan meeting?"

"It's normal procedure. It gives us a few moments to make sure everything is in order. Also when we enter the clan meeting, having the three of us together will give us a stronger presence."

* * *

Tabitha was just slipping on the emerald green sweater she'd picked up on their shopping spree when she heard Raja's voice. Ty had already discussed the meeting with her, and he was just going over the same things with Raja. Knowing there was no reason to rush, she did a double-check of her makeup.

There is no reason to be so nervous. These people want me here, or they wouldn't be going through so much to make me feel at home. Ty wouldn't have come across the country if I didn't belong here. The pep talk was doing nothing to calm her knotted stomach. Biting the bullet, she joined the men, hoping she could keep her nerves a secret.

"Tabby, we need…"

Ty's words stopped as she strolled into the living room. "Sorry."

"You're fine. They can't start without us. I just wanted to get a move on." He placed her hand in his. "Tabby, there is nothing to worry about. They're happy to have you home, but you won't have time to mingle with them now. We need to take care of business, and the clan can get back to preparing for tonight's festivities. If you want to be nervous about something, be nervous about the party. With everyone demanding the Queen's attention, you might end up with a jealous mate." He laughed before kissing her.

* * *

The conference room was a large, open room with a slightly higher platform that dominated the area. It was nothing like she'd expected. In the conference rooms she had been in before, there was normally a large table with chairs surrounding it. *I guess when you have forty members, it would be hard to find a table large enough.*

In front of the platform, the chairs were set up in two rows of five with a walkway between them. The members were already there chatting amongst themselves when Tabitha, Ty and Raja entered.

Already on the platform was a man, looking worse for wear, wearing only jeans and heavy iron chains on his wrists and ankles. Two guards stood on either side of him. She assumed it was Hunter.

Tabitha's stomach went from knots to doing flip-flops as Ty, still holding her hand, led them toward the microphone. "The first order of business is to introduce you to your Queen. After too many years, Tabitha has returned home as my mate."

Everyone dropped to their knees. "Welcome home, Queen Tabitha," the audience chorused.

Ty stepped back, allowing Tabitha to access the microphone. "Thank you, I'm pleased to be among you. I look forward to speaking to as many of you as I can tonight. Those I don't get to tonight, I promise you will have your turn. I want to get to know each and every one of you."

"Now we have other business to attend to." Ty turned toward the guards. "Please bring Hunter forward and have him take his place."

The guards brought the prisoner in front of Ty and Tabitha, and Hunter kneeled in front of them. "Hunter, you have been charged with changing in front of a human and murder. Do you have anything to say for yourself?"

Hunter looked at them with such hatred in his eyes, causing Tabitha to suck in a harsh breath. “I don't know what happened. I think she drugged me. I never would have done this otherwise. I…”

Before he could continue, Ty brought up his hand, silencing the man before them. “Raja thought you might say something like that. There were alcohol and drug tests done on you after your capture. They were clean. You were not drugged. You just let your emotions take hold of you, and this is not the first time. Therefore, as punishment for this crime, you will be unable to change for the next six months, and you will be confined to the cell downstairs until the collar is removed. After that, you will have no contact with humans or leave the compound for five years.” Ty gave a nod to Raja.

In an instant, everything changed. Raja stepped forward with the collar. Hunter, knowing his fate, didn’t want to go down without a fight. He went after Ty, attacking in human form, because with the chains, he couldn’t shift. Ty pushed Tabitha out of arm’s reach, toward the guards.

One guard moved in front of her to keep her out of the way as the other one took her arm, trying to drag her away from the scene. She wanted to help Ty, but she couldn’t shift yet.

“I won’t leave him!” she told the guards, watching as Ty and Raja became tigers, leaving their clothes torn to shreds.

“My Queen, there is nothing you can do. You need to be somewhere safe.” Felix came from the crowd to her rescue.

She shook her head no, and Felix didn't fight her. He stood in front of her, ready to protect his Queen if the fight shifted their way.

Tabitha felt helpless as the action unfolded before her. Claws ripped through flesh, sending blood splattering across the stage. Hunter was powerless to fight off two shifted tigers. Ty had Raja helping him, but her heart was in her throat. As they took Hunter to the ground, he went after Ty's neck, leaving him no choice but to take a fatal bite from Hunter's neck.

Hunter stopped moving, and they changed back. Ty quickly scanned the room until he found Tabitha next to Felix. His shoulders relaxed, clearly relieved when he found her standing with Felix.

Ty turned to the clan. "Don't make Hunter's mistake. I have never put up with this kind of behavior, and I will *not* start now. That is showing no respect for your Queen. Now we will retire to our quarters, and we'll see you tonight at the party."

Neither man seemed bothered by their nudity as they crossed the room toward Tabitha.

Coming to stand in front of her, Ty wrapped his arms around her, pulling her against him. "Are you all right?" he whispered.

She nodded, not trusting her voice. She held on to him as though he were the last life raft in a turbulent sea.

"I would like to see you in my quarters in twenty minutes," he said to Felix before he excused the man.

As they headed toward their quarters, Raja followed behind, waiting until they were away from the other members before speaking, "If it's all right with you, I would like to shower and put on some clothes."

"That's fine. I have Felix coming in twenty minutes. I would like you there before he arrives, if possible." Raja nodded, and Tabitha followed Ty down a side hall.

As the door closed, Ty wrapped his arms around her again, squeezing her so tightly she could barely breathe. "Ty…"

"I'm sorry, Tabby. I just needed to feel you in my arms." He lessened his grip slightly. "These new feelings that come with having a mate are all new to me. I wanted to make sure you were safe, but I had to take care of Hunter before he hurt someone else. My emotions were torn, but I had to do what was right for us and the clan. You didn't get hurt, did you?"

"No, Ty. I'm fine. Felix and the other guards tried to get me out of there, but I didn't want to leave you."

"Next time, promise me when there is danger, you'll let the guards defend you or get you out of there. Don't be hard-headed."

"I was in no danger. You and Raja had Hunter under control."

Ty took a step back from her, allowing her to see his face and the grave expression upon it. "I'm serious. Things could have gotten out of control today. You're the Queen of all Tigers and the only true bloodline left. You need to be protected."

"I might still be human, but I'm not helpless. I know when to get out of the way. Stop worrying about me so much."

Ty refused to back down. "You don't know how vulnerable you are to the clan, and to me. You are irreplaceable. You don't understand what lengths people like Pierce will go to, to kill you."

"I do understand. I know if I'm killed, the tiger shifters will die. Trust me, that scares me. I have never been responsible for something so big. I might not have gone through the change yet, but I'm not just a normal human either. Come on, you need a shower before they arrive."

"Won't you join me?" Ty kissed her neck.

"Oh, what the heck."

Chapter Fifteen

Raja sat on a chair speaking to someone on the phone when they entered. Cutting off whoever was on the other end, he said, "I'll call you back."

He stood, slipping the cell phone in his pocket. "I apologize. There was a problem with Hunter's sister."

Ty lowered himself to the chair and brought her with him. "Are you needed to deal with her?"

"Thomas is taking care of it. She's distraught over what happened to her brother and is in a state of grief. They were very close. After he was arrested, she confided in me that Hunter had changed. She couldn't put her finger on it, but there was something different about him. They were growing apart. She asked me to help her brother. I explained to her it would be up to you what happened and most likely, he would get the help he needed. She thinks I betrayed her."

"I expected her to be upset, but Hunter left us no choice. You don't attack your Alpha and get away with it. The punishment for attacking your Alpha and losing is death. There is no way around that."

Raja nodded. "Everyone knows this, and if she were thinking clearly, she would understand, but grief does strange things to people. I had the doctor give her something to calm her. She needs to rest. I'll speak with her soon, but this is not why we're here."

"Very well. I asked you here because after today's incident, I've decided to assign around-the-clock guards. One of those guards I have chosen is Felix. I'm planning to promote Felix to Captain of Tabitha's Guards. Felix has done a great job as one of my guards, and I trust him to keep Tabitha safe. Today he came from the back of the conference room, where he was stationed, to get her out of the way. He understands she must be kept safe. Even though Tabitha is a stubborn, hard-headed woman and refused to leave the room," he paused giving Tabitha a pointed look, "he kept her out of danger and was ready to protect her if needed."

"I think he would be perfect for the job. Felix is one of the few I would trust with my life. Who else do you have in mind?"

"I haven't decided on anyone else yet. I wanted Tabitha to meet the rest of the clan. We'll see who fits well with her, who seems like they would be a good match. I would like four guards assigned to her, at least two at any given time. Most of the time, I'll be around her, but if something happens like it just did and I have to take care of it, I want to know she'll be safe. I won't have her put in danger. I want the guards to keep her safe when I can't."

Tabitha leaned away from Ty to look at him. "Don't I get a say in this?"

Ty rubbed the top of her hand that was resting on his leg. "Baby, I'm doing this to protect you. You can have some say on *who* will protect you. But you are my mate, and I would rather risk you being mad at me for who I choose than not have the guards that can keep you safe when I can't."

"I'm safe. I don't need or want guards protecting me. I'll be fine." *I'm not a possession he must keep under lock and key.*

Ty looked away from her, toward Raja. "Could you excuse us for a moment?" Ty grabbed her hand and stood, pulling her along with him. He led them into a room off the living room that appeared to be an office, with deep burgundy walls and the same hardwood floors as the rest of the quarters. A large L-shaped desk, as neat as the rest of the house, dominated the center of the space.

"Tabby, I know you don't want this—you've made that clear—but it's something you need. I will not have you in danger, and there will be times I won't be able to protect you like I want to. You need this, and it's normal for the Alpha and his mate to have guards. I have my own guards. Stop being stubborn and accept this."

"I don't want people following me around all the time." She crossed her arms, not caring if she appeared petulant.

"They won't be. While we're in our quarters together, they'll either be off on their own or outside the door if the threat level is high. If you come into our quarters alone, they'll have to do a walk-through to make sure no one is here, but they won't stay in here unless you're in immediate danger. They will only be with you when you're outside our quarters. If we need to, we can set up more boundaries later, after you go through the change. I just want to make sure you have the guards you need when we need them."

"Okay, you win on this one for right now. But once I go through the change, we'll discuss this again."

"Thank you." Ty leaned down to kiss her. "Now let's finish this."

They walked out of Ty's office. Felix was now in attendance.

"Felix, thank you for coming." After they took their seat again, Felix and Raja also sat.

"Felix, Tabitha and I have decided we would like you to be the Captain of her Guards. Are you interested in this promotion?"

"That's such an honor. Thank you both. I would be honored to accept."

"Thank you. We'll let you know soon who the other guards will be. We haven't finalized those yet. Until then, you'll be protecting her along with Thomas, from my guards. Before I assigned any long-term guards, I wanted her to meet the clan. Within the next few days, you'll know and can start training them. You can explain the new changes to Thomas, and I want both of you to meet us here at six o'clock tonight to attend the party."

"Yes, sir." Felix rose and appeared to be awaiting dismissal.

"That's all for now." When the door firmly closed behind Felix, Ty turned his attention back to Raja. "Until Tabitha goes through the change, I want you and the rest of the guards on call twenty-four hours a day. I want the compound security on alert. If anyone comes on the grounds, I want to know, and if that person is not permitted to be here, then I'll hold whoever is on guard at fault. I won't have Tabitha at risk, no matter how small. Things are dangerous now."

"I'll inform the clan. If there is anything you need, please let me know." Raja rose, understanding the conversation was over.

"I still don't think I need guards. I can protect myself."

When they were alone once again, Ty growled. "Tabitha, I have never felt this way about anyone before. I want you safe, even if that means you're mad at me. You mean everything to me."

"Ty, you're the first person who has ever really cared about me. I…" her voice broke, all the blood rushed to her head. "I love you. If you want guards for me, then that's what I'll have. I was just upset that you didn't talk to me about it first. I should have a say in this kind of stuff."

Ty leaned down, put one arm behind her legs and one behind her back, and carried her off to the bedroom. He kissed her neck as he walked. "You're my mate. It's my job to protect you."

"I'm not a china doll. I don't want to be protected." She let out a frustrated sigh.

"I want you safe."

Tired of fighting, Tabitha wrapped her arms around Ty's neck. "I'm not used to someone wanting to protect me. I'll try, but I'm not some little school girl who can't stand up for herself. I might not have the physical strength and speed you have, but I'm not a dainty human either."

Ty laid her gently on the bed. With her arms still around his neck, she leaned up into his body, kissing him deeply, drinking from his lips, as she gently pulled him onto the bed. Gliding her hands down his tight, toned chest, she stopped for a moment to feel his biceps, and she was glad to have him all to herself…at least for a little while.

Ty tugged off her shirt before slipping his hand behind her back to unhook her bra as she explored his chest and arms. Tossing the discarded clothes to the floor, he kissed her neck and made his way down her chest, taking extra time at each nipple. He gently took the nipples into his mouth one at a time and sucked ever so softly, then released it and rolled his tongue over it. He looked up at her with so much devotion shining in his eyes, making her heart flutter.

The fire between their bodies was like a hot summer night in Mexico. Their hearts threatened to pound out of their chests; their palms were sweating. Ty's strong hands caressed every inch of her body. She moaned in ecstasy. He was tender as he memorized every curve of her body with his hands and mouth. He took his time tasting each and every inch of her, sending shivers of fire throughout her body.

Ty gently and lovingly kissed down her stomach and stroked her thighs all the while. With every touch, her body cried out for more. It was like she couldn't get enough of him. His hands sought out the special central core of her body, while the heat and wetness drove her crazy.

He took his time caressing and kissing her body. She could feel their tigers calling to each other, urging her to hurry, while the human part of her wanted to take this slow and cherish every moment together.

His fingers delved inside her. As he worked his fingers, her body moved with the motion. He kissed the inside of her thighs. The passion drove the fire through her—fire like she'd never felt before. He made his way to her core. He licked lightly over her sweet spot, flickering over and over, nearly driving her over the edge. She grabbed his hair and moaned with extreme pleasure.

Tabitha rolled him over, laying him on his back. She placed another deep kiss on his lips while she caressed his chest, taking care to feel every chiseled muscle, licking and kissing as he writhed in pleasure under her.

She knelt on the bed in front of Ty, wanting to show him the love she felt for him. She caressed his flesh, stroking him and stoking the fire inside him. She licked the length of him and slowly took him into her mouth. Ty threw his head back in pleasure.

Tabitha enjoyed the feel of his hands running through her hair as her actions excited him.

"Come here." He tugged on her hair.

Moving up the bed, she angled herself to allow him access. As he entered, she cried out with pleasure. The thrusts were deeper and faster, but not too fast. Both of them moved with such precision, as if it were a well-choreographed dance. Their bodies rocked back and forth until they exploded together in unison.

Breathless, they laid there hot and sweaty, cuddled together, not wanting to move, their legs still entwined.

Ty lifted his head enough to kiss her. “I love you, Tabby.”

Chapter Sixteen

Tabitha was in the middle of the custom-made bed that dominated the bedroom, snuggled deep in the warm comforter, still trying to wake up.

"I didn't think we would sleep that long. We should get ready for the party." Ty tossed back the covers before slipping out of bed. He turned around to find she hadn't moved. "Come on, you can't be late for your own party." He smiled down at her.

With a moan, she scooted to the edge of the bed. The floor was littered with red, black and silver throw pillows they'd tossed off earlier. Grabbing one, she threw it at the back of Ty's head. "If it's my party, they can't start without me."

"Love, you don't know these tigers. They love to party."

"Are you sure everything will be fine tonight? Maybe with what happened today, we should postpone it." She bent to pick up the pillows.

"Tabby, this is something the clan has been preparing for since I told them you would go through the change and I was going to try to bring you home. We cannot deprive them of something they worked so hard on. This means a lot to them." As he spoke, he walked around the bed to where she was and took her hands. "Everything will be fine. I promise."

"I know. I just worry they won't like me."

"How could they not like you? You're amazing in every way." Ty tilted her head up with his large hands and before she could respond, he kissed her.

* * *

Standing in front of the mirror, Tabitha admired the dress they'd bought in Pennsylvania. She pulled her hair into a French twist, allowing a few curls to escape and hang down. She was adjusting the black and red beaded belt when she heard Ty talking to Raja and the other guards in the living room.

I never had a reason to dress up before. I feel like a princess…I guess I should feel like a Queen instead. She chuckled to herself as she did one more quick take before stepping out of the bedroom.

As she came into view, everyone became quiet. She could have sworn she could hear the air sizzle with shifter magic. The men were dressed in black tuxedos and looked as if they could be on the cover of a magazine. No one moved for a moment, then Ty came forward. “My Queen, you look marvelous, absolutely mind-blowing. Let me introduce you to the guards for tonight.”

They walked over to the men standing in the front entrance. Three of the men where kneeling, while the other two, Raja and Felix, stood a step behind. “These are Thomas, Leo and Korbin. They are our guards for this evening.”

Our guards? Or did he really mean my guards? I’m leaning towards mine. Quick catch of the tongue there, mate.

Ty gave her a slight nod, letting her know she was to smell each of their necks. They smelled the same way Felix had when she’d first smelled him, but it wasn't as overwhelming anymore, because the smell was all around her now that she was in Alaska.

Weird, but now that I think of it, my body isn’t sore, and I have felt fine since arriving. Ty mentioned I would feel better once I was around my own kind, but he didn’t mention it would all just go away.

“Welcome home, my Queen,” each of the men said as she kissed their necks before they stood. Inside their tailored jackets, she could see the butt of the guns they wore. The shock must have showed on her face, because Raja stepped in front of the other men, took her hand in his and kissed it. "If I may, my Queen, you look stunning."

"Thank you, Raja. You look pretty good yourself."

"Men, she is to be protected at all cost. If anything goes wrong, get her out of there and somewhere safe. Felix, I'm placing you in charge of keeping her safe. If anything happens to her, I will hold you personally responsible. I don't care if it is so much as a paper cut, your ass is mine." Ty laid a hand on the small of her back, directing his attention at her. "I want you to listen to them. If they feel the area is unsafe, go with them."

Tabitha didn't fight him. She just nodded. Ty wasn't doing this to make her appear weak. There was too much at risk, and she had to think of the livelihood of the tiger shifters as a whole. "Shall we get this over with?"

"It won't be that bad. Come on." Ty took her hand as they left the quarters, surrounded by their guards.

Chapter Seventeen

The dome was normally used for training when the weather outside was nasty, but tonight every inch of it was party central. The clan had constructed a ballroom floor in the middle, complete with a DJ playing tunes. The entryway had a large arch that was covered in black and gold balloons. On the far right wall, it said *Welcome Home, Tabitha* in big gold sparkly letters. Everything was done in black and gold. The tablecloths were black with white and gold plates; the wine glasses had a gold rim around the top. The lights were low and on every table, candles glowed, giving a romantic flare to the dome.

There were buffet tables going all the way down the left wall and a large white and gold cake at the end of the buffet. Waiters walked around with glasses of champagne and other drinks.

"This is amazing." She stared, trying to take it all in.

"It's all for you. They're ecstatic to have you home with us again. Come, let's get a drink and then mingle with everyone."

Ty stopped one of the waiters and took two glasses of champagne from the tray he was carrying. Raising the glass to take a drink, she became aware they were starting to draw a crowd. Raja and the guards tried to surround them to keep the clan back a little, but they were on them before the guards could close the circle.

A loud growl exploded next to her before she heard Ty yell, “Stop this right now!” Everyone went still around them. “I don't know what has gotten into everyone, but it needs to stop now. I know you’re excited to meet Tabitha. So here is what we will do. I want everyone to go sit at their tables. Tabitha and I will come around to each table and spend a few minutes with you. Later, after we’re settled, Tabitha will have more time to meet with everyone. However, tonight, we’ll take some time out to meet with everyone, and then we would like to enjoy this wonderful party you have been so generous to throw in her honor.”

People spread out, moving to find seats at one of the six tables placed around the dome. The guards went to their predetermined spots, except Raja, who stayed with them.

They started with the table to the left, allowing them to make a complete circle and end up at their table by the dance floor. Each table was eager to talk with her, making her want to stay with them as long as she could. But Ty kept her moving from one member to another, promising they would have more time with her soon, and that Tabitha wasn’t going anywhere.

"I know you want to meet the needs of each member, but don't wear yourself out tonight. You have plenty of time," Ty whispered in her ear as they headed to the next table.

She nodded. *That is easier said than done. How can I rush through everyone when they are so kind and threw this party for me? I wish I could stop time and spend longer with everyone.*

As they went around the room meeting the members, she noticed a number of men with the golden auras. There were two that stuck out to her. One of them was Marcus, Tora's husband, and the other one was Lance.

Lance was at the first table, and he seemed on alert and ready to take action if something happened. His deep forest green eyes seemed to take everything in while still looking relaxed.

* * *

After going from table to table, they were finally able to sit down and enjoy their dinner. Ty had mentioned earlier they had some of the best chefs as part of the clan, and she wasn't disappointed with the meal. The salmon was delicious.

"Are you having a good time?" Ty asked as they finished dessert.

"The best time of my life." A huge smile plastered itself on her face. She leaned in closely and whispered, "But there are a few people I'd like to talk to you about later." She had questions about the people with the golden auras around them, but it wasn't something they could talk about with people within hearing range.

"You met Lance tonight," he said, motioning toward the first table. "He is one of my guards. I gave him the night off to spend with his new mate. This allowed him to enjoy the party and for us to have guards that would devote their full attention to any problems that might arise this evening. He is a good guard, but the mating bug is hard on everyone."

Tabitha loved how Ty was able to slide in the information she wanted without it seeming out of place or raising questions from anyone who might have overheard.

A young girl, no older than fourteen months, came running toward them. Her wobbly legs barely held her up; her long hair was the color of rubies bouncing behind her as she ran, until she tripped, falling down hard. Before the first tear fell, Tabitha was on her feet, heading toward her.

"It's all right, sweetie." Wrapping the little girl in her arms, she wiped the child's tears away.

The little girl's knee was bleeding, so Tabitha balanced the child on her hip as she grabbed a napkin from the table to wipe the blood. She realized then that when she'd jumped up to help the little girl, she'd spooked the guards. Felix and Thomas were the first to respond, at her side before the rest realized what the commotion was. Ty watched from the table, a smile on his face.

“I’m fine,” she told Felix and Thomas before returning her attention to the girl.

Raja must have also come to her aid, because he was standing behind her. “Here, Tabitha, I can take her.”

The child was clinging to her neck when Raja tried to take her, and she wouldn't let go.

“Can you believe that's my niece, and she won't come to me? I'll get her mother.” Raja let out a soft laugh before strolling off into the crowd.

“That's Tora and Marcus' little girl, Scarlet. I’ve never seen her go to someone she didn't know, and she loves being with Raja. She’s just full of surprises tonight.” Ty sat there with a twinkle in his eye.

“Is that true? Do you like me, Scarlet?”

The little girl merely sat in her lap as happy as could be.

“She must, because she never goes to anyone. We had to have our babysitter in a dozen times before we could leave them alone together, because she would throw a fit something terrible. Tonight the babysitter is sick, so she had to come along with us. I’m sorry if she has been any trouble.” Tabitha looked up to find Marcus standing in front of her.

“She’s been no trouble at all. She is a darling little girl.”

Marcus tried to take the girl from her lap, but she held strong to Tabitha's neck.

"She's fine here if you want to leave her for a bit."

Marcus looked to Ty, as if not sure what to do. Ty gave Marcus a slight nod. He accepted it and went to rejoin his wife.

"You're amazing. Everyone is so taken with you, just like I said they would be." Ty wrapped his arm around her shoulders.

"I guess I had nothing to worry about. Everyone is so friendly and so accepting. I can't help wondering what it would be like to grow up with a group of people like this, people to call family." As they were talking, Scarlet curled up in her lap as though she were going to take a nap.

* * *

"May I have this dance?" Ty stood, taking her hand.

Tabitha nodded, rose, and placed the still sleeping Scarlet on the chair.

"I'll watch her. Go dance and mingle," Raja said when she caught his eye.

There were only a few people dancing, leaving them with most of the floor to themselves.

After the song ended, one of the female tigers she'd met earlier stepped up to the microphone. "If I could please have everyone's attention." She waited for everyone to quiet down. "Ty would like to say a few words."

Felix came to stand next to Ty as they went to the microphone. "First, I would just like to thank you for this wonderful party that you put together for Tabitha's homecoming. I'm ecstatic to have such a wonderful woman as my mate. We're blessed to have her back among us and as our Queen. Thank you, Tabitha, for coming home, and for trusting us. I love you."

Before she realized it, she was heading toward Ty, tears clouding her vision. As he stepped to her, she wrapped her arms around him. "I love you too," she said and kissed him.

Chapter Eighteen

Ty and Tabitha were dancing around the room when Raja came up to them. "Excuse me, but may I cut in?"

Ty nodded and stepped back, allowing Raja to take over dancing with her. Ty moved off the floor toward Felix. While Ty spoke to Felix, Raja leaned into her body and whispered, "Ty is a whole new man with you in his life. I have never seen him in such high spirits. He loves you more than he could ever put into words. Never doubt that."

Tabitha felt her cheeks heat with embarrassment. "Everything changed in just a matter of days. Everything feels so overwhelming, except when it comes to Ty. I love him; he has been my rock though all of this. Discovering we're mates was more than I could have hoped for."

When the song ended, Raja stepped back and still holding her hand, he kissed the top of it. "It was a pleasure. Thank you for this dance."

"I thought you could use this." Ty held out two glasses of champagne.

"Thank you."

Ty handed her the glass as they walked off the dance floor. "What bad things did Raja tell you about me?"

"Wouldn't you be interested in knowing?" She laughed before taking a sip of champagne and gave him a sexy but innocent smile.

Ty gave her a very serious look, which she returned with another laugh. "Come on, Ty. It was nothing. Would Raja honestly say anything bad about you behind your back? You two seem so close."

"We're close, but I'm sure he would tell you some dark secret if he thought he could get away with it."

Before she could tease Ty for worrying about what Raja had told her, a large tiger limped onto the dance floor. The tiger was covered in blood and obviously in terrible pain.

Tabitha took a step toward the tiger. "Tabby, stay back. He doesn't smell familiar. He isn't of our clan."

The guards gathered around Tabitha, keeping her away from the tiger.

"I can help him. You know I can."

"This is against my better judgment." He reluctantly agreed to her request, stepping aside so she could approach. "Form a protective circle around her, but keep her out of arm's reach."

Ty and Felix stood in front of her, closest to the tiger, leaving her only a small view between their shoulders.

Her power was still new to her, but she knew she would be able to hear the tiger if she could concentrate. She took a deep breath, trying to relax. "Can you tell me your name?"

Before the tiger could answer, someone from the clan yelled out, "What does she think she is doing? How is this going to help us? He's in tiger form. He can't answer her."

Ty turned, shooting the man a look that could kill. "Did you forget you don't contradict your Alpha? She's of her father's line. Her gift is telepathy. Now shut up and allow her to help him."

She could hear the rustle of people moving around, trying to get a better look. It was breaking her focus, and she could barely hear the tiger's thoughts. "Okay, Lukas, why are you here?"

You're really your father's daughter and can read my thoughts?

Tabitha nodded.

I mean no harm to you or your clan. I came to warn you. There's a traitor in your mist. My clan intercepted a message that was meant for Pierce. I need to speak with you and Ty alone. I have the proof you need. You can't mention this to Ty in front of everyone. The traitor will hear you. Tell everyone except Ty I was traveling through the area when I was attacked, which is mostly true. If rumors are true, you should be able to concentrate and send the message to Ty.

Tabitha concentrated really hard. *Ty, can you hear me? Please hear me.* Wanting to leave the impression that she was still speaking with Lukas, she kept her gaze on him but focused her attention on her mate.

Ty looked at her as if he were about to say something but was hesitant.

Tabitha tried again. *Ty, can you hear me?*

Finally, a response. *Tabby, I can hear you but I don't know if you can hear me?*

I can hear you, Ty. This is so freaky. Listen, I'm going to tell the clan that he was hurt passing through. He has information about a traitor within our clan. We need to speak with him alone, without the clan.

Okay, Tabby, but explain to him that our guards will be in the room.

Before giving the cover story to the clan, she focused back on Lukas. *Ty has agreed to speak with you, but our guards will be in the room.*

Without turning her back on the injured tiger shifter, she raised her voice, allowing everyone to hear her. "Clan, he was passing through the area when he was attacked by a hunter. He managed to get away but is badly injured. My guards will escort him to the infirmary, where our doctor will look him over. Ty and I will make sure he gets the best treatment and is settled in. Enjoy the rest of the party."

Chapter Nineteen

For the doctor to care for the injuries on Lukas, he had to shift back. This also allowed them an easier time speaking with him. Lukas shifted into a boy no older than seventeen. His boyish looks gave his age away, his short red hair had a slight curl to it and his face showed the slight sign of learning to shave. His voice was soft and crackling, just like it had been in her head.

"Boy, where are you parents?" the doctor asked as he stitched the boy's wound.

"I'm alone."

"We'll speak with the boy when you're finished," Ty explained when the doctor didn't seem happy about the answer.

After the clan doctor was finished looking Lukas over and had gotten him settled into a bed in the infirmary wing, Ty turned to the doctor. "You will not speak of this to anyone. They're not to know the boy's age or injuries. If you're asked about him, tell them to speak to me. Understand?"

The doctor nodded.

"Korbin, please escort Doc back to the party. Except Raja, I want the rest of you to wait outside the infirmary. Tabitha and I will speak to the boy alone."

Leo and Thomas started toward the door, but Felix didn't move. "With all due respect, I don't think you should be alone with him. He may not be safe."

"Are you choosing to disobey a direct order?" Ty gave Felix a threatening look, as if to let him know it wasn't a good idea to push Ty at this time.

Felix looked from Ty to Tabitha. Tabitha tried to convey the message to Felix not to do this.

"I apologize. I mean no disrespect, but as Captain of the Queen's Guards, I'm in charge of keeping her safe. I don't know how safe this situation is."

"Not only are you disobeying an order, you're suggesting your Alpha cannot protect his mate." Ty's face was red with anger. She could see his body starting to vibrate with the magic that brought on the change.

Felix stood in front of Ty, not willing to back down, but visibly shaken. It was written on his face that he knew this might not end well. If it came down to a fight, he knew he wouldn't win against his Alpha. "That's not what I meant. I just..."

Ty interrupted Felix, "Get out of my sight now!"

Felix didn't try to explain or make Ty understand. He just turned on his heels and walked out the door to join the other guards.

"I can't believe that boy!" Ty turned to her, the anger still showing on his face.

"Remember, you did tell him earlier that if anything happened to me, it was his ass. He just wants to make you proud of him." She touched Ty's arm.

The touch of her hand was enough to calm him, and he nodded. With Ty calm, she turned to look at the boy, who appeared so small and fragile in the large hospital bed. "Please explain to us how you got this information and who the traitor is."

"When my father was killed by Pierce's gang, my brother took over as Alpha of our clan, and since then we have been after them. We intercepted a message that was sent from your clan to him, saying that Tabitha had finally joined your ranks and had mated with the Alpha here." Lukas tried to sit up straighter in bed, but he was clearly in pain.

"Who sent the message?" Anger returned to Ty's voice.

"The name was Chris."

"Are you sure?"

"Yes. I have the proof with me." The boy looked at her and then back at Ty.

"What do you mean you have it? You were in tiger form, and you didn't have a bag with you." She eyed him questioningly.

"I hid my bag before I got here in case something happened and I was searched. I didn't want anyone to find it before I had a chance to speak with you. On my way here, I was attacked and had to change into tiger form to get away. I'm sorry I forgot to explain that. If you could send someone you trust for my bag, you'll have all the proof you need. I can tell you where I placed it, but I don't think I could make it there in this condition."

"Where is the bag?" Ty asked, already forming a plan, judging by the thoughtful expression on his face.

"It's in the basement of the North Pole apartment building in the rafters to the left of the heater. It's a black backpack."

"Raja, take Thomas and see if you can find this bag. I want to settle this."

* * *

While Raja and Thomas went to retrieve the bag, they continued to question the boy.

"What clan are you from, Lukas?"

"My brother took over the West Virginia Tiger Clan. Our numbers are small, but we are a tight group. My father was friends with Tabitha's father. We felt after he was killed and then my father was killed, it was our duty to keep an eye on Pierce whenever we could. Hopefully, this would allow some warning if he was planning an attack."

"We have been trying to keep an eye on Pierce as well."

A knock sounded from behind them. "Yes?"

"We found it." Raja entered with a black bag draped over his shoulder.

Ty took the bag and set it on the bedside table. Unzipping it, he found a laptop.

"We found a way to hack into his cell phone and record his conversations. On there is a message that went to his voicemail. Luckily, we were able to intercept it, deleting it before he received it. Since I've been traveling, I can't be sure that he hasn't been contacted again," Lukas explained.

"Bring the message up." Ty handed the laptop to the boy.

He flipped the laptop open and hit the power button. The laptop booted up quickly. He clicked a few buttons before the message started playing.

"It's Chris. Tabitha is on the red-eye plane back tonight. The clan is planning a celebration for her homecoming. You want her dead, then I need backup to take her down. I did what you asked. Now you better pay up."

Goosebumps covered Tabitha's arms, and her stomach sank. Ty put his arm around her, drawing her into him.

"We'll handle this. Lukas, you have to understand our situation. Until this situation is under control, we are going to have a guard with you. No cell, computer, nothing. You brought this to our attention, and we appreciate it, but we have to be cautious this isn't a trap."

"I understand. If you could contact my brother to let him know I'm here, I'm sure he would appreciate it. I'll cooperate in any way I can."

Ty nodded, turning to Raja. "Gather the guards including Marcus, Lance and Milo. I know they had the night off, but we need them. We meet in our quarters in ten minutes."

Chapter Twenty

Tabitha paced the bedroom, trying to get her feelings under control. Sure, she knew Pierce was after her, but this was making it set in. Pierce was *seriously* after her and wanted her dead. *How do you handle someone wanting you dead whom you've never even met?*

"Tabby?" Ty came into the bedroom.

"I'm fine. I just needed a moment."

"Come here, baby." He wrapped his arms around her. "We'll take care of this. I won't let anything happen to you."

"I know." His face was full of doubt, making her continue. "Honest. It's just sinking in that he wants me dead. I've never even met him, and he wants me dead." She was still having a hard time wrapping her mind around it.

"I know, but it is going to be fine." There was a knock on the door to their quarters, meaning the guards had arrived. "Felix, grab the door. We'll be out in a moment."

She closed her eyes and took a deep breath, trying to gather all the courage she could. She wouldn't break down. "Let's do this."

"I can handle this myself if you want a few minutes."

"I'm fine. I just want it over with."

He ran his hand down her back one last time as they went to face the guards.

"Please have a seat. This is going to take some time." Ty led her toward a chair that was angled between the two couches, giving her a good view of everyone.

Even with the crowd in the living area, it didn't seem confining. There was still room to move around, as if when building it, they knew there would be a dozen people here waiting for their orders.

"Most of this won't come as a shock to you…Pierce knows Tabitha is here and is most likely on his way." He gave them a moment as if he wanted to let that sink in. "I want everyone on high alert. I want the compound locked down like Fort Knox. No one on or off without my knowledge. Felix, I want guards around the clock on Tabitha. You can arrange that, but as Captain of her Guards, I want you in the main compound. You can take the guest quarters."

Felix nodded.

"Next order of business: Thomas and Leo, I want you to find Chris Knight and escort him to one of the cells. I'll deal with him shortly."

"Yes, sir. Charges?" Thomas asked.

"Treason. Conspiracy to commit murder."

Thomas and Leo left without another word. The rest of the men watched their sovereigns, waiting for their orders.

"Marcus, Lance, you have first guard duty. The rest of you, we will be discussing your shifts and get back with you shortly. In the meantime, keep this to yourself. You're dismissed."

As the guards filed out, Marcus and Lance rose to take their posts at the entryway. "Lance, I want you to inform the guards at the gate we are on lockdown. They are to call me if anyone tries to enter or leave. Then change out of your tuxedo and return here."

"Yes, sir."

"Marcus, wait a moment. Felix, you need to hear this also. Raja, unless you have something pressing, I'd like you to stay."

The men didn't move. They waited patiently for whatever Ty was going to throw at them. Tabitha, on the other hand, shifted nervously in her chair. She knew what Ty was going to tell them, and she couldn't help but wonder if they would feel differently toward her.

"Some of you know about the legends, the ones surrounding Tabitha. I trust you to keep this between us. It is true that Tabitha must carry on her line or tiger shifters will cease to exist. She has to be kept alive at all cost."

"Understood," Felix said.

"There's more…Tabitha will unite all tigers."

"What?"

"Marcus, I know Tora has told you the legend that a female tiger will come along and unite the tiger shifter population."

"Sure, but it's just that, a legend."

"This proves it isn't." Ty grabbed the book from the shelf they'd laid it on and handed it to her.

"You already know I have the gifts from my father's line. Why is it so hard to believe?" She touched the book, and it sprang to life. "I'm supposed to choose three more guards to stand at my side through this. Ty and I have already discussed that we would like the two of you to be a part of it."

"Raja is our Lieutenant and while he remains, we still need three others. We would like the two of you to be a part of that. Felix, as the Captain of the Guards, you needed to know the complete situation. Marcus, I'll be up front with you—this will be dangerous and will put not only you but your family in danger. But being Raja's family, the danger will already be there. It is up to you if you wish to pass on this position. However, no matter your decision, you will not be allowed to speak of this." Ty laid his hand on her shoulder, gently rubbing it.

"I'm honored to be a part of this and will do whatever I can," Felix said.

"Marcus?"

"Yes. I'll do it. Who will be the third?"

"We haven't decided yet. I wanted Tabitha to get to know each of the guards a little more. At this time we are leaning toward Lance. Since he will have first shift, I'm hoping Tabitha can talk to him a little longer and get her own feel for him."

The men seemed satisfied with the answer. Tabitha yawned. The excitement was taking its toll on her.

"Felix, why don't you work up a schedule for the guards and then you can finish enjoying the party if you wish. Plan another meeting with the guards for tomorrow morning after breakfast. We need to go over a plan for dealing with Pierce."

"Yes, sir." He stood, ready to leave.

Marcus and Raja didn't move, as if they understood Ty wasn't finished with them.

"Ty, I know it is against the protocol, but I think Tora should be informed." Raja rubbed his hand over his head.

"He's right." She turned to face Ty, who was still standing behind her. "With both Raja and Marcus standing with us, she will be in danger. It's not just her that we have to worry about, but Scarlet also."

"Okay. Marcus, retrieve her from the party and return here."

Chapter Twenty-One

Tabitha had changed into her plaid pajama pants and tank top and was stretched out on the couch when Tora came in, carrying a sleeping Scarlet.

"I was wondering where the party went."

"Have a sit, sweetie." Marcus took the sleeping child from her, giving her arms a break.

"What's going on?"

"Tora, come sit with me. We just want to talk to you." Tabitha slipped her legs under her, giving Tora room to sit next to her.

"What's going on?" Tora eyed everyone suspiciously, lowering herself to sit next to Tabitha. Marcus still stood, softly rocking Scarlet.

When no one else took the lead, Tabitha stepped up. "Tora, we asked for you to join us to explain some of what happened tonight and some changes that will be happening."

"We are telling you this because Raja and Marcus have both agreed to be a part of the operation, and there is danger involved. We want you aware so you can take precautions for you and Scarlet." Ty leaned against the armrest beside Tabitha.

"What danger could we be in?"

"Marcus and Raja have taken a new position…" Tabitha took a deep breath before continuing, "They tell me you know the legends of the female tiger shifter that will come from my line and unite the tigers."

"It's a legend my parents passed down to us." Tora nodded.

"It's not a legend. It's true. Tabitha is the one," Raja finally spoke from the window he was looking out.

"How do you know this?"

"She can open the book of her line, she has her father's gift and it's what our parents always told us."

"Okay. But why does this place us in danger? Dad never made it sound dangerous."

"Tora, he told it to us as a bedtime story. If he made it sound scary, do you think you would have been able to sleep?" He ran his hand through his hair. "Pierce won't be the only one gunning for her. Once this is out...Sorry, Tabitha, but it is true."

"I know, Raja. Tora, this will also place you in danger. With both your brother and husband as part of the chosen guards, it could make you a target." Tabitha watched Tora closely.

"Chosen guards?"

"The book said I must choose three guards to help with the tasks. Raja, as our Lieutenant, will stay in that position. I have chosen Marcus and Felix, and we are considering a few different people for the final position."

Tora nodded as she sat, taking it all in.

"No matter the situation, you're always in danger, being my sister." Raja moved closer to her.

"True. What can I do?"

"There is nothing to do at this moment. But we wanted you to understand the situation and be on your guard. If there is ever a time we feel the danger level for you is high, we will assign you guards. We will do everything we can to protect you and Scarlet," Ty said.

"Thank you. Scarlet is my main concern."

"We understand." Tabitha laid a hand on her knee.

* * *

"He has been detained." Lance strolled through the door before he realized they were not alone. Tora still sat on the couch.

"Who?" Tora asked.

"I'm sorry, sir."

"You know better than that, Lance. However, Tora has been informed of some of the situation. Being Raja's sister, she is in more danger than most." Ty turned to Tora before continuing, "Chris Knight. He is charged with treason and conspiracy to commit murder."

The shock she felt was written clearly across her face. "Chris…" she murmured under her breath. Tabitha wouldn't have heard it had she not been sitting next to her.

"Were you close?"

When Tora didn't answer, Raja spoke up. "They dated a while ago, before Marcus came to the clan."

"We drifted apart once Marcus and I were mated, but I always hoped he would get his life together and find his mate."

"Would it be all right if I walk my wife back home and put Scarlet to bed?" Marcus asked.

"Just don't be long." Ty nodded. "When you return, take your position at the door."

Marcus reached for Tora's hand and pulled her up. He wrapped his free arm around his wife and left.

"Lance, take your position outside the door until Marcus returns. When he does, we would like to speak with you privately."

"Yes, sir." He nodded to Ty before taking his post.

The three of them were quiet for a few minutes before Ty broke the silence. "Raja, if you ever wanted to step down from your position as Lieutenant and start your own clan, now is the time to do it."

"I have no desire to leave. This is my home."

"Good. I wanted to get that out of the way before things were set in motion." Ty rubbed Tabitha's shoulders gently. "I've been giving this some thought while Tora was here. Pierce's men are stupid enough to attack us here, so I want us to be ready. I think they will attack tonight after the party when everyone is exhausted. If I'm wrong, tomorrow we'll see if we can stage something."

"I agree. Which is why I think you need more than two guards."

"Fine. After the party, gather up some of the men and station them around the compound. I want them to be ready at a moment's notice, but I want the place to appear as if everyone is in bed. I don't want them to know we are expecting them."

Raja nodded at the same moment Lance opened the door.

"If this is a bad time, I can come back."

"No, Raja and I were just leaving. Keep Tabitha company until I return." Ty kissed his mate's cheek. "I'll be back soon."

Chapter Twenty-Two

Tabitha ran her hand down Ty's chest, her head resting in the crook of his arm, as the compound began to settle around them. She knew there were guards ready to defend them, but her heart was still in her throat as the possible outcomes ran through her head.

"What did you think of Lance?"

She knew he was trying to keep her mind off what might be coming for them, but it wasn't helping. She felt helpless, and sitting here doing nothing was killing her. These people were after her, not the clan, but her clan was ready to fight to their deaths for her.

"I liked him. He seems to always be on guard. As if he is picturing the worst case scenario and is ready for whatever comes his way."

"Being ready for the worst-case makes you ready for whatever happens. He is a good guard, and I believe he would make our core group stronger. He takes orders well and thinks outside the box."

Tabitha nodded.

"Then we agree on Lance?"

"What about his mate? Does she get a say in this?"

"Each mated pair is different. Some consider their spouse in the decision, and some do not. Marcus knows Tora well and knew he didn't need to seek her opinion before accepting. It isn't normal for the guards to be able to discuss situations with their mates. Assignments are normally on a need-to-know only basis. If Lance wishes to decline the position, that is his right, however, with the current situation, he will not be able to discuss it with his mate until it is made public."

"You mentioned mating hormones before. Do you think Lance's head is on straight enough for this?"

"That is a concern. I think he would be perfect for the position without the mating hormones. Now that he is newly mated, his thoughts are on other things." To show what he meant, he kissed her neck. "Then what do you think of Thomas?"

"He takes orders well." Tabitha let out a soft moan as Ty continued to kiss her neck. "I can't think if you keep doing that."

"That's the whole point."

He slipped his hand under her shirt, ready to tear it off, when his cell buzzed. "Damn it!" He reached for the phone, growling. "This better be good." He snarled. "Okay. Stand by until they make their move. Don't let them escape." He hit a button and was silent for a moment. "Raja, they're approaching. Get Felix. I want you both over here."

"Ready for this?" Ty slid the phone back into his pocket.

"Not in the least bit, but what choice do we have?"

"Have you ever handled one of these?" he asked, pulling out a 9MM Glock.

"I've never shot a gun before."

Ty had just finished showing her how to work the gun when she heard someone open their door. Ty had instructed everyone earlier to leave the lights off, giving the impression they were asleep.

"It's just Raja and Felix," he whispered. "You're going to be fine. Just remember to stay behind us, and if Felix tells you it's time to move, you move, no questions asked. I don't care what's happening to me, you go with him. I'll find you when it's safe." He leaned down until their foreheads were touching. "I love you." He kissed her.

"Felix, if anything happens to her...." Ty growled.

"She will be safe. I'll protect her with my life."

The bedroom door opened, and everyone braced for action. There was a good chance whoever was on the other side of the door wasn't friendly.

"It's Thomas," came a whisper as the door inched open.

"What the hell are you doing, Thomas?"

"I saw Lance leave his post, and I wanted to check it out."

"Shut the door. I'll deal with Lance later. Where's Marcus?"

"He's still on watch. They were heading this way." Thomas closed the door behind him.

"Then we better be ready," Ty said, eyeing Felix, who nodded.

Something tumbled to the floor in the living room. Everyone's body went stiff as they readied for what was coming. Ty and Felix moved to stand in front of Tabitha, blocking her view of the door, while Raja stood at Ty's side and Thomas next to Felix.

If the time comes, will I be willing to shoot to kill and save myself? She wasn't sure of the answer, but still, she held the gun to her side, while the men had theirs aimed at the door.

The door splintered as the intruders kicked it in. So much for picking the lock.

"Stop right there," Ty hollered when shadowy figures entered the room.

The faint light coming in the window allowed Tabitha a glimpse of the face of the youngest man in the back of the group before he turned as if to run but found Marcus and another guard blocking the door.

Ty let out a deep growl as the two other intruders went for their weapons . "Raise those guns and you will die."

"Either way, we will die. It is better at your hands than at our Alpha's." The two men in the front weren't going to go down without a fight, while the last one looked terrified.

Tabitha couldn't take her gaze off the last guy. There was something about him. Almost as if he weren't there willingly. Before she could question it further, all hell broke loose.

In a split second, she heard Felix turn the safety off his gun as two of the intruders shifted. The third one stood there, apparently not knowing what to do. Felix pushed her back against the wall as Raja and Thomas shifted to be on equal ground as the others.

Ty braced himself, ready to protect her if they got past Raja and Thomas. Marcus already had the other man detained, cuffed and on the ground outside the bedroom. He left the other guard to keep watch over the prisoner and came to assist with the others.

Growls echoed around the small space, and hair flew through the air as they attacked each other. It was hard to know which shifter was who. She recognized Raja. There was a different energy around him that she was able to distinguish from the others.

Her heart skipped a beat as one of the tigers was thrown against the wall to land in a heap on the floor, where he didn't move. She could see the tiger's chest rise and fall with shallow breaths, but if he was not moving, he had to be seriously injured. *Don't let that be Thomas!*

The fighting went on for what seemed like hours, but could have only been minutes. Tabitha's heart was in her throat as she watched people fight for her, knowing that if it wasn't for her, this wouldn't be happening.

A second tiger fell to the ground, his throat ripped open. As he died, he shifted back to human form. With one dead and one severely injured, Raja and Thomas shifted back, allowing Tabitha to breathe easy.

Chapter Twenty-Three

"Finish him," Raja ordered, handing Thomas a gun before slipping on one of the pairs of shorts that Ty grabbed for him and the others.

Without hesitation, Thomas took the gun, walking toward the injured tiger. Tabitha tried to make herself call out, to tell Thomas not to do it, but she couldn't. The tiger in her knew this had to be done.

A shot pierced the night, and her breath caught in her throat. Tonight, as she'd embraced her tiger, she realized part of her human beliefs had died.

"It had to be done. He was here to kill you. There is no way we could have trusted him after that." Ty put his arms around her, drawing her close.

She nodded, resting her head on his chest, breathing in his smell.

"I want to speak with the prisoner."

"Tabby, I think that can wait until morning."

"No, I need to do it now."

He nodded. "Raja, allow him to sit. She can talk to him before he is taken to a cell."

Before Raja could react, his cell phone rang. Pulling it out of his pocket, he answered it. "Yeah?"

"I'll deal with the prisoner," Marcus said as Raja moved way from everyone to take the phone call.

"The grounds secured? No other intruders on the premises?" There were a few moments of silence as the person on the other end answered. "Good. Send out a search party. Follow his scent. I want to be notified if you find anything." Raja ended the call.

"Thomas, help Marcus. Close the door behind you." Raja slipped the phone back into his pocket.

When the bedroom door was firmly closed behind him and only the three remained, he explained, "There was someone down in the cells. Chris is gone, and the guard is dead."

"Shit! I didn't question him yet."

Tabitha decided to share her knowledge. "I don't think he would have been any help. But I think the one in the living room has information." The men eyed her inquisitorially.

"What gives you that impression?" Raja spoke when Ty didn't.

"I watched him. He knows something. He didn't want to be here but had to be. If I can speak with him, I think I might be able to find out whatever he is hiding."

"Raja, go ahead out there. We will be there in a moment. I want to speak with my mate first."

* * *

Tabitha sat on the corner of the bed, with Ty kneeling before her. "Explain to me this feeling that you're getting."

"It's hard to describe. There is like a nagging feeling in the pit of my stomach. Sometimes I can just tell something," Tabitha tried to explain.

"I think you might be coming into another gift."

"What do you mean?"

"As mates, we are able to feel each other's feelings. You shouldn't be able to pick up on others'. But I think you are. This is one of the abilities that some of the members in your line have." Ty stood, raking his hands through his dark hair.

"But I already have my ability."

"It's possible to have more than one. Maybe you'll have whatever ones you need to bring the tigers together."

"We don't have time to question this now. Let's deal with the situation at hand, and then maybe we can consult the book. Maybe there is some kind of answer in it." Tabitha took a deep breath before standing.

Chapter Twenty-Four

In the living room, the man slouched on the couch. His head hung, and tears glistened in his eyes. The guards standing beside and behind were ready to leap into action, if the situation called for it.

"I don't think we need everyone here," she whispered to Ty.

"Everyone except Raja, Felix and Marcus, resume your duties. We have this under control now."

"Thank you," she murmured to Ty. Marcus stood behind the couch, while Felix watched from the side, and Raja and Ty stood by her side.

For the first time, she was able to get a good look at the man before her. He was in his early twenties, young, and if her impression was right, he was a new shifter. But there was an odd smell to him. It wasn't as if he'd just come from another clan, but as if he was entirely different.

"What is your name?" she questioned the man sitting before her.

"Connor, ma'am."

"Why?" The sorrow poured off him, almost drowning her in it.

"Why what?"

"Let's start with why are you here? What led you to this point? You didn't act like the others."

"I'm here because I was ordered."

"Ordered by whom? If you were ordered, why didn't you attack like the others?"

"You already know by whom. I didn't attack because none of this is about me. I didn't have anything to do with it and didn't want to be a part of it. I have nothing against you and see no reason you should be killed. Yes, I know his reason for it, but then he should be doing the dirty work, not sending others out to do it."

"If you don't believe in the cause, then why are you out here fighting for him?"

"Because I have no choice."

"Everyone has a choice." She could feel his sorrow mix with anger.

"I didn't."

"Why not?"

"It's a long story."

"She is trying to save your life, and you don't even have the decency to answer her questions. Answer her or the guards will escort you to your cell while we decide your fate," Ty growled, his patience growing short.

"One of his…Pierce's followers murdered my mother a few years ago. He took me under his wing and gave me a place to live. I knew someday there would be a price to pay for it, but I never expected he would want me to kill someone for him."

"What about your clan?"

"Mom was sort of a lone wolf."

She finalized realized what she smelled. "You're a wolf."

It was more of a statement than a question, but still, he answered it with a nod.

Ty took a step forward, earning him a look from Tabitha.

"Wolves are a dangerous breed," he said as if that explained the step.

"I know some find my kind to be unstable, but I mean no harm to anyone. I tried to find a way out of the situation, but they were under the order to kill me if I didn't complete the assignment. I thought I could find a way to get away from them, but up until we entered the bedroom, I was smashed between them."

His words vibrated the truth through the room, touching her core. Ty didn't seem convinced, or maybe he wasn't taking any chances, but he still had his body angled in front of her, ready to protect her.

"You had to know Pierce was dangerous before now. Why stick around him all these years?"

"Dangerous, yes, but all shifters are dangerous to a point. Certifiably insane is a whole different ball game."

"Why did you stay?"

"It wasn't until recently I understood how crazy he is. I had a job offer and was supposed to leave a few weeks ago. I thought I would have been done with him then."

"Then why are you here?" Ty growled.

"When I told him about the job, he nearly killed me. I just recovered."

"What can you tell us about Pierce's plans?" Tabitha touched Ty's arm, trying to calm him.

"I don't know what you did to him, ma'am, but he will stop at nothing to see you dead." Sorrow shone in his eyes.

"I didn't do anything to him personally. It is more about who I am." Ty shot her a warning look, and she knew better than to go into details. "What are his plans? Where is he staying?"

"He didn't tell me his plans. Only that he wanted you dead. They're staying in a cabin on the mountain."

"Give us directions. We need to locate him." Ty motioned to Raja, who seemed to understand the silent communication.

Raja grabbed a pad and pen from the desk and handed them to Connor. "If you make any attempt to escape or to place any of us in danger, we will kill you. There will be no questions." Raja uncuffed his hands, allowing him to write the directions down.

"Understood," Conner said as he rubbed his wrist before picking up the pen.

Will going after Pierce and his team threaten the family I found? Will someone die in my place?

Chapter Twenty-Five

"The men are on their way to the location. They'll call when they have the suspect in custody. Connor, if this lead is the truth, you might have earned your freedom," Ty said as he and Raja returned from the debriefing conference room.

Connor stayed silent as if he were considering his own fate. Tabitha knew he was wondering if he was going to die that night. He didn't have family or friends who would miss him, but he had dreams that he wanted to accomplish before it was his time.

"Connor, I want you to shift into your wolf…" Tabitha didn't get to finish, as Ty cut her off.

"Absolutely not!" he shouted at her.

"Ty—"

"There is no way that is going to happen. He's more dangerous in animal form. I will not have it, not with my mate in jeopardy."

She moved closer to him so they could discuss it calmly between themselves. "Ty, I might be able to sense more than he could tell us. Something that only his subconscious knows."

"It's too dangerous."

"He won't harm us."

"You don't know that. This could all be a trap." Ty stood with his arms across his broad chest, staring down at her.

"I can feel that he is telling the truth. He means me no harm. You know this could help us. Let me do it before it's too late, before Pierce has a chance to escape or make a move."

"You are my mate. I'm supposed to protect you at all cost. This isn't protecting you."

"You trusted me with Lukas; trust me now. We can take precautions if that makes you feel safer." She laid her hand on the arm still crossed over his chest. "I wouldn't put myself in danger for the hell of it."

"Raja, Felix."

The men came to stand next to them.

"Against my better judgment, I'm allowing this. We will stand in front of her. If he makes a move, kill him."

The men nodded, and Ty turned around to face Conner. "Go over to the corner over there. I want you far enough away from her. When you shift, lay on the floor. If you make a move, you will die."

Connor moved into place, removing his clothing when he reached the corner. Ty touched her cheek. "My mate, I love you."

"I love you too." She stood on her tiptoes to kiss him as he wrapped his arms around her.

"We're ready," Raja said from behind them.

"Let's do this before I change my mind."

"Shift when you're ready." Tabitha stood protected by the men. She had a spot between Raja and Ty that she could see through, but it was like being behind a wall and only being able to see through a small window.

The magic gathered in the air as the boy transformed in front of them. A gasp escaped her lips as she saw Connor's life play out before her. Ty watched her from the corner of his eye but when she nodded, he turned his attention back to the wolf.

Tabitha closed her eyes, giving full attention to the memories of his life. It wasn't until the recent memories of Pierce that she could feel his anger. Not at Tabitha and her men, but at Pierce.

Pierce tortured the boy at every turn, making his life hell. She finally understood why he'd stayed. No other pack would allow him in now that he was associated with Pierce, for fear of problems.

She saw his memories of what happened before he came to the compound. Everything he'd said to them was true, but seeing them, she was able to realize things he didn't. There was a suitcase sitting by the door in his memory.

Any idea where he is going? she mentally asked the wolf.

She didn't get a sense he understood what she meant. His memories continued to play out before her, leaving her the impression that he didn't see the suitcase.

"Pierce is gone. You won't find him at the cabin. He left some of the others behind but took his key people with him."

"How do you know this?" Ty asked.

"There's a suitcase in his memory, next to the door. When Connor walked in, there were bits and pieces caught. I don't think he put them together, but I did."

"So he told us the truth about his involvement?"

She didn't answer, just nodded as she saw another house in his memories. This house had bad memories, and she could tell he didn't want to go back there.

"Whose house is that?" Then she saw both his mother and Pierce. "You can shift back."

But nothing happened. Connor laid there in wolf form, not moving.

"He can't," Raja said as she began to wonder what had happened.

"Oh, hell. I forgot you mentioned weaker shifters aren't able to shift back. Why was he so willing when he knew this would happen?"

"I don't think he thought he had a choice. You're an Alpha. Even outside his pack, he understands authority. I'm sure if he didn't know it before, once Pierce came into his life, he knew it," Ty said, moving to give her a little more room to see between him and Raja.

"But I have questions I want him to answer." She sighed. "It's different than with us. He has to think of the image or memory."

Ty gave a little squeeze to her hand, letting her know that she shouldn't go on. "It's the best we can do right now. He won't be able to shift for at least another few hours."

She sat down on the couch and ran her hand through her hair. She was drained, and it was going to take time and patience to get the answers she wanted.

"Connor, you showed me a picture of Pierce and your mother. I don't understand how they owned the house. Was there something between them?"

He shook his wolf head and showed her his mom, coffin and then Pierce.

"Pierce took it over when your mother died."

He let out a howl, as if to tell her yes.

"How did your mother know Pierce? She had to know him to leave him the house, and for him to take you in."

She wanted direct answers, but all she was getting were bits and pieces of things. Her brain was too tired to put the puzzle into a whole. She rubbed her temples, trying to figure out how everything went together.

"Tabby, why don't you get some sleep? You can question him more when he changes back."

"What will happen to him while I sleep?"

"He will be made comfortable. Once he shifts back, he will be tired and need to rest also. But when he wakes, you can continue this. This is not helping you when you're tired. You're just going to stress yourself out." Ty sat down next to her.

"I don't want him in the cells," she whispered.

"Tabby…"

"No, they know where the cells are. I won't risk losing him back to their hands."

"He isn't a stray dog that you can find a new home for," Ty said roughly.

"I never said he was. He needs help to get out of the situation, and I want to help him. He is giving us information. It's the least we can do."

"Least we can do." He snarled. "Did you forget he was on the team that came here to kill you?"

"No, I didn't forget, but he didn't. He surrendered to Marcus."

Ty let out a deep growl. "Woman, you're going to be the death of me."

"Just put him up in one of the guest rooms with guards, then we will both be happy. He'll be secure and comfortable."

He just stared at her before nodding. "Raja, arrange it."

"You won't do anything stupid that makes me regret this decision, will you, Connor?" His mind told her his thoughts were already on a nice, comfortable bed. "Connor, focus one more time. There was another man with you tonight. Who was it?"

She saw a picture of an older man with gray hair and a limp. The man lived a hard life, and if the memory was correct, didn't look as though he had long to live.

"Any idea who it was?" Ty asked.

"I see the man, but I don't know who he is. I'll ask him about it later."

"They are ready for him," Raja said, getting off the phone.

"One last thing. Did you know Chris?"

Nothing came to his mind. "Ty, do you have a picture of Chris? Maybe he doesn't know Chris by name but by face."

He grabbed the picture of the clan from a nearby shelf. "Last one, second row on the right. But you're not getting near him to show him."

She grabbed the picture out of his hands and set it on the floor, halfway between Connor and the door.

"On your way out, look at the picture." She moved to Ty's side.

The wolf trotted toward the door, stopping at the picture. Memories flooded her mind, of him and different people, but she couldn't make sense of it.

"Think about it and we will talk about him and everything else when you wake."

He howled in frustration. She could tell there was something he wanted her to know, but he couldn't get it across to her.

Chapter Twenty-Six

The next morning, Connor woke feeling refreshed. He hadn't slept that well in ages. For the first time in a while, he didn't have to worry about someone coming in to kill him while he slept. He wasn't constantly checking over his shoulder for Pierce. There was a weight lifted from his shoulders, allowing him to breathe easier, even if it was only for a bit.

He wasn't an Alpha and never had the desire to be. After his mother's death, he'd wanted the comfort and security of a pack but because of Pierce, no one would accept him. He was a lone wolf, and lone wolves didn't survive long.

Pierce took him in, gave him a place to sleep and put food in his stomach, but Connor never was a part of the pack. Connor did it out of loyalty to his mother. *Loyalty. What does Pierce know about loyalty? More like guilt. Guilt over getting her killed.*

He lay in bed, knowing there was a guard just outside his open door to make sure he didn't try to escape. *Whatever they do to me, it's better than what Pierce would do if he found out I was still alive. How will I ever get myself out of this situation? Maybe if I can help them…* He racked his brain, trying to figure out a way to help.

The man in the picture from last night, he recognized him. Chris. He got wrapped up in this mess to save his stupid sister. *Didn't they say he was taken from one of the prison cells?*

Knowing Pierce, that meant Chris was dead. He wouldn't let someone survive who could hold something over him. Without Chris, his sister didn't stand a chance.

Chris? Maybe he is the key to all of this. If he was anything like his sister, he would have kept records.

Jumping out of bed, he slipped into his jeans that someone had remembered to grab. Zipping up, he found the guard standing in the doorway. "I need to speak with your Alphas."

"They will speak with you when they're ready."

"Trust me. I have information they need. Please, just tell Tabitha I asked to speak with her."

The guard unclipped his phone from his belt and hit a button. "It's Adam. He's awake and demanding to speak with her." He ended the call. "She will get the message. Just hang tight. There's a television out here if you wish to watch some while you're waiting."

He hated waiting. It made him want to climb the walls, but he knew there was nothing he could do. Forcing the situation wouldn't help.

* * *

"He's awake and wishes to speak with you," Felix said, filling Tabitha's cup of coffee.

"Finally." She let out a sigh of relief.

"Finish your brunch, mate, and then we will have him brought in." Ty eyed her over his e-tablet as he read the reports from the guards.

She was still in her plaid pajama bottoms and tank top as they enjoyed their brunch. Ty had kept her in bed long after they woke. She'd enjoyed the early morning sex and cuddling, but she wanted answers. Rolling her eyes, she popped another strawberry in her mouth. "I'm done."

"Mate, you are the most impatient woman I know." Ty shook his head. "Have Raja escort him in."

She stood from the kitchen barstool and moved closed to him. With his attention still on the reports, she kissed his neck. "We have a few minutes," she whispered after getting the soft purr she loved.

“I need more than a few minutes. You will get your answers, and then you’re mine for the rest of the day.”

“Maybe I have other plans.” She took his earlobe into her mouth, gently sucking on it.

“You’ll forget all about them. Remember what I told you about mating heat. I can’t get enough of you. I walk around with a constant hard-on. I need you.”

She could smell them coming down the hallway. “Soon, baby, soon.” She leaned down and kissed him.

“Not soon enough for me,” he rumbled.

After a quick knock of warning, the door opened. Raja ushered Connor to the couch.

“Morning, Connor. I hope you were able to sleep well,” Ty said as they joined him, sitting on the opposite couch.

“Very well. Thank you.” He ran his hand over his knee. “I’m sorry I wasn’t able to convey the message you wanted last night, ma’am.”

“Jumping right in, I see. Good. The man in the picture…from your reaction, I assume you know who that is.”

“Chris. Yes, I know of him.”

“Of him?” she questioned.

"To be clearer, I met him only once, but I knew him through his sister."

"When he joined our clan, he told us he had no siblings," Ty stated.

"Then he lied to you. His sister got wrapped up in some bad stuff a few years ago: drugs and what have you, but then she got with Pierce."

"Got with Pierce? What do you mean?"

"It's unusual for shifters, but you could say she is his girlfriend."

"Shifters don't really date like humans do. They might go out on a date or two while waiting to find their mate, but it isn't the same as when humans date. Born shifters have mates. When we find our mate, we know it and pursue it. But before that, there is no reason for a relationship. We can get our needs met or go out, but relationships are something that is rare. Mainly for the reason of why do it if there is no future for the two of you," Ty explained.

"But Pierce isn't a born shifter." Tabitha said, trying to understand how that would relate to Pierce.

"True. There are very few bitten shifters, so it isn't a proven fact, but it is believed that they do not have mates. They are just like the rest of the human population. They have to find the one they want to be with."

"Okay, but what does this have to do with anything? We're after Chris."

"I think the reason Chris betrayed you is for his sister. She mentioned to me before that she wanted to get away from Pierce but couldn't. I believe Chris and his brother, Mike, thought he could exchange the information about you for his sister," Connor said.

"Mike?" Tabitha squealed, feeling queasy at the sound of the name.

"He could have come to me. We would have helped him with his sister." Ty growled.

"Mike lives in Pittsburgh, from what I hear. He visits his sister monthly. They are close."

Could it be the same guy? It can't be a coincidence that Alice was dating a man name Mike.

Ty obviously was thinking the same thing she was. He pulled out his cell phone, hit a few buttons and pulled up Mike's wanted picture, before showing it to Connor. "Is this Mike?"

"Yes. What's he wanted for?"

"Murder . . . He murdered my best friend, Alice. When the police went to arrest him, they found his apartment vacated. If he knew who I was, why not turn me into Pierce? My life should have gained his sisters freedom."

Connor shrugged, leaving the silence hang heavily in the room.

She pushed it aside, for something to deal with later. "But why lie about siblings when he joined the clan? You said he has been here for years," Tabitha pointed out, trying to get the complete picture.

"They lost touch for many years. He thought she was dead until last year, when she reached out to him for help."

"I'm not an asshole. He could have come to me. There was no reason to betray me and my mate."

She laid her hand on his leg. "I'm sure he didn't see a way out of his situation, and when he traded the information, he didn't know I was your mate."

"He knew who and what you were," Ty hollered. "I will see him dead for this."

"I'm sure Pierce already did that." When they both just stared at Connor, he continued, "You said the cell was empty. There is no way Pierce would have let him live. He would have assumed that he knew too much. I'm sure he is dead."

"Then what information did you tell the guards we would want to know?"

"His sister keeps records of everything. I know she sent him letters and things. I think if you search his personal belongings, you will find something that might be useful."

"Why do you think any of it would be useful?" Tabitha asked.

"If anyone knew anything, it would be her. She is the closest person to him. If he trusted anyone, it would be her without a doubt. Let me help search the room. I know her smell. I might be able to find anything that is there quickly."

Chapter Twenty-Seven

Tabitha was stuck in the compound with Felix while Ty and the others went to search Chris's cabin. Time went slowly, like watching paint peel. She understood why Ty wanted her to stay here, away from the danger. There was no telling what they would find in the cabin. It might be booby-trapped for all they knew.

"I can't take this." She growled and walked to the window again to see if she could see anything.

"Relax. They will call when they find something."

"I hate waiting."

"I'd never guess." Felix's words were laced heavily with sarcasm.

She gave him a look to let him know she wasn't amused, but he just chuckled. She could hear a faint ring. *What is that? My phone.*

She raced to the bedroom, where her purse was, and pulled the cell from it.

"Don't!" Felix yelled at her.

Not listening, she hit the talk button and put it on speaker. She had a feeling she knew who it was, since the one person that called her was dead. "Hello?"

"You escaped my grasp again, but know this: Ty can't protect you forever. When I catch you, you will suffer all the more for making me chase you." The voice came through the speaker phone.

"Then let's put an end to the games. Where are you?"

"You don't think I'm that stupid, do you? I know you would bring your guard dogs. But don't worry, we will meet again and soon." With that, he hung up. She tossed the phone back in her purse.

"Shit!" Felix stood behind her, growling. "We should have put a trace on your cell, but we never thought he would call it."

"I'm not sure he'll call it again but to be safe, do whatever has to be done so we can trace it next time."

"We should let Ty know." He reached for his own cell.

"There's nothing he can do about it. It can wait until he's finished. He needs to concentrate on what he's doing. We can't allow them to be distracted and miss something."

Felix nodded.

* * *

"He what?" The anger rolling off him nearly buckled her knees.

"Just as she said, he called her cell phone while you were gone," Felix told him again, helping her to the window seat. "Control your anger. Look at what it's doing to your mate."

She could feel him trying, but his anger was out of control. "Come here," she bit out.

Ty sat beside her, and she wrapped her arms around his body. As they touched, the anger started to subside.

"Her phone should have been set up for us to trace the call."

"No one thought he would call, but I'll have it set up right away. Either way, she handled it well. You should be proud of your mate," Felix explained.

"I am. But I want her safe." He pulled her into his lap.

She didn't fight, because she wanted to touch as much of him as possible. "I'm safe. Did you find anything?"

"Connor and some of the guards are going through what we found. There were many letters from his sister and what appears to be a notebook in which he kept records of his contacts with Pierce. I came over here to get you. Pierce must have never considered there would be evidence, or he would have destroyed them."

"Well, let's go. I want to see what we can find."

* * *

After spending hours going through the letters and other things that were recovered from Chris's cabin, they still had no idea what Pierce's plans were. They knew where they might be able to find him, different houses and locations that he used in the past; places he preferred, contacts he had, a number of the people in his clan, but still no closer to stopping him.

"Wait, what about this Jessica?" Tabitha asked from her position on the couch as she read through one of the notebooks.

"Jessica?" There was surprise in Connor's voice.

"You know her?" Ty asked, catching the disbelief in his voice also.

"Not really know her but know *of* her. It's his sister. She's human, but she knows about shifters and Pierce's condition. If anyone would know his plans or where he is, it's her. She isn't supportive of his decisions, but still, he confides everything to her. He wants her to accept his life and approve of him."

"Thomas, see what you can find out about her—location, habits, spouse. I want to know everything you can find."

"I can help. I'm a master at computers and finding things people want to stay hidden," Connor stated, somewhat quietly.

Ty didn't answer right away but looked at Tabitha, who gave a small nod. "Okay. Go with Thomas. If you two find anything, I want to be notified immediately."

Chris followed Thomas out of the conference room with a look of determination on his face.

"Now the rest of you, I want you to finish going through this stuff. Same thing stands. I want to know if you find anything. Tabitha and I will check in later." He reached for her hand. "Come on, mate."

She laid her hand in his, and he smoothly pulled her to her feet. She eyed him uncertainly. He led her out the door, Felix following behind them.

"I want you. You're my mate, and I'm tired of waiting," he whispered, nuzzling against her neck.

Chapter Twenty-Eight

They made it to the bedroom in record speed. Tabitha was ready for him. The heat and need vibrated through their bodies.

He slipped his hand under her shirt and pulled it over her head. "Mine."

She ran her hands through his hair, moving it away from his eyes. She loved to look into his eyes. It was like looking into his soul. There was so much love and compassion there.

"You have too many clothes on." She pulled at the gun shoulder-holster he wore, sliding it down his arms.

"Too slow." He jumped out of bed and stripped out of his clothes before she could blink. "Now *you* have too many clothes on."

She slipped out of her pants. "Better?"

Running his hands over her body, he purred with satisfaction. The heat between them was growing, becoming overwhelming. "We waited too long."

Beyond words, she let out a hum.

"With the mating heat, if you wait too long, it's harder to control the beast within. It will be rough."

"I don't care. Just take me."

"I won't be able to control myself," Ty snarled, his body tense next to her, letting her know he was trying to control his own beast.

"I love you for who you are. Man, tiger and all. Nothing will change that. Please, Ty, don't make me beg. I want you."

Without hesitation, he slid into her core, making her moan with pleasure. He roared, shaking the walls. This time, there was no exploring of each other's bodies. Their need had full control over them.

Her lips touched his, and a spicy taste drew her in. Their kiss was fast and furious as if matching the pace as he slid in and out of her core.

A moan of desire escaped her lips, and her eyes closed as she soaked in the pleasure that surrounded her.

"Open your eyes, Tabby. I want to watch your desire build."

She opened her eyes as her body arched. Her lusty needs came forward to match his urgency.

Her nails dug into his back as ecstasy found them. His release was announced with a roar.

He slipped out, rolling to lie next to her, their legs still tangled. She curled into him, her head on his chest, and listened to his heavy breaths. Her leg draped over his as they enjoyed the after-bliss.

“I didn’t realize it before, but our marks come alive when we’re together,” he said, raising his hand so she could see.

The tattoo glowed a faint gold light, as if there were a light bulb beneath the skin.

Interesting. “Why do you think that is?”

“I don’t know. But it’s fine with me as long as more don’t keep appearing,” he stated with a laugh.

“One is enough for me.”

“Tabby, before you sleep…”

Opening her eyes just a crack, she looked up at him.

“I think Thomas should be the third chosen guard. I know you liked Lance also, but after last night, he isn’t trustworthy. I still need to deal with him running off to be with his mate.”

"I agree about Thomas. We'll tell him later. Why did Lance go to his mate? Did he think she was in danger?" She ran her hand over his chest, feeling the tight abs under her fingers.

"I wouldn't be so upset about it if that was why. But that isn't the case. He was horny. Since it was quiet, he thought he had time to get his needs met without anyone noticing him. He didn't see Thomas coming as he was sneaking away."

"What will you do to him?"

"He will be suspended from our guards and required to work the perimeter. He'll also have to work with a partner to keep an eye on him until we can trust him again. If he screws up, the punishments will be more severe. Or if things would have gotten out of control last night and you were injured, he would have been at fault. I don't think he realizes that if last night you would have been injured or killed, I could have demanded his death."

"His death because someone else harmed me?"

"Yes. Guards have the duty to protect their charge, or you, in this case. If they fail, then they will be held accountable. It's the way of the shifters."

Chapter Twenty-Nine

They were spending so much time in the conference room, it was starting to feel like a second home. Whoever designed the place should have had it connected to Ty's quarters instead of in a space down the hall. At least the walls were a cheerful yellow, giving a light and airy feel even if there were no windows.

Thomas and Connor sat across from them in the debriefing conference room. Raja and Felix stood close to the door.

"Connor found the sister. It was buried, but Jessica is living in California. She is attending college there for her PhD—you'll never believe this—for animal psychology." Ty looked over the notes on Jessica as he debriefed the guards.

"Very good. With any luck, she will be of some assistance to us. We'll have to get someone go check her out," Ty said, his hand resting on Tabitha's leg.

"If possible I would like to assist whoever goes. I have met her and might be able to help. She knew my situation and felt sorry for me. She tried to tell me to get away from Pierce before it was too late. If she is going to open up to anyone, I think I have the best shot," Connor stated in an unsure voice.

"We will discuss it and let you know. You have been a great asset to us, and we appreciate it. My mate believes you mean us no harm and will not betray us. If you are inclined to stay on, we would gladly provide you with a cabin of your own."

"Thank you." Relief washed over Connor's face. "I'd like to do what I can to help you and your clan take down Pierce."

"We appreciate that. I think your computer skills might be of great use to us." Ty took a sip of coffee. "Connor, if you could give us a few minutes to speak with Thomas, then he can show you to Guest Cabin One."

Connor rose and walked toward the door. She could feel his emotions playing havoc on him. He was thankful for the chance Ty was giving him, but she could also feel his fear that he was placing more danger on them.

"Connor, I'm really glad you will be staying with us. There is no need to worry any longer. You're safer here than anywhere else," Tabitha said as his hand closed around the door handle.

He nodded and closed the door behind him.

“Thomas, last night you proved yourself worthy of protecting Tabitha. I’m sure you know the legends that a female tiger will come and unite all tiger shifters.” Ty didn’t wait for an answer. He just dove in head first. “They’re true. Tabitha comes from a long line of strong tigers, and she will be the one.”

“I suspected she was the one. My understanding is there hasn’t been a female from her line in generations.”

“Great, then we don’t have to drag this out. We have been tasked with finding three guards to help us with this transition, and we would like you to be a part of the team. There’s no use lying. It will be dangerous, but there will also be rewards.”

“I’m flattered. May I ask who the others are?” Thomas placed his hands on the table and leaned forward.

“Marcus and Felix are the other two choice guards. Raja will remain our Lieutenant throughout and once the transition is complete. The next step will be put into motion soon but for now, this must go no further than this room.”

“I understand. If there is nothing else, I’ll show Connor to his cabin.” Thomas pushed back his chair and rose.

“That will be all. Once you’re done, you may have the night off. Get some rest. You have guard duty in the morning.” Ty stood as well.

"One last thing. I think you made the wise decision in allowing him to stay. His technology skills will be a great advantage for us." Without another word, Thomas was gone, leaving a heavy silence in the room. Raja and Felix stood, waiting for Ty to make a move.

"Could you give us a moment?" Tabitha asked as Ty paced.

The men opened the door, stepping through before shutting it again.

"What's wrong, Ty? I can feel your uncertainty racing through you." She went to him and wrapped her arms around his waist, hoping to bring him some comfort.

"I'm questioning who to send to speak with Jessica. Raja is the most convincing and most likely our best shot of getting information out of her. But he is also my right-hand man, the one I would trust to keep you safe if something happened to me."

"Nothing is going to happen to you, love. But I was thinking you should send Leo. At such a critical time, I don't think any of the key people should be far apart. Keeping Raja, Felix, Thomas and Marcus near for the next stage is what I was thinking. If we need to send in reinforcements, then send Raja. Let Leo and Connor go scope out the situation, and we'll go from there."

He lifted her, making her wrap her legs around his waist, then kissed her—long, deep, passionate kisses that made her want to rip his clothes off. A moan escaped her mouth.

"Soon, my love. First, we must finish business." Without letting her go, he hollered, "Raja!"

Raja opened the door and peeked in. "Yes."

"Find Leo and tell him Connor and he will be leaving tomorrow night to speak with Jessica. Fill him in on the situation and then make the arrangements. He has seventy-two hours to find her and get the answers we need from her."

"Yes, sir."

"Also let Felix know to stand guard, and we do not want to be disturbed unless there's an emergency."

Raja closed the door, and Ty continued where he left off. He tugged her sweater over her head, growling. "Mine. All mine."

"Always yours. I love you, Ty."

ABOUT THE AUTHOR

Born and raised in the Pittsburgh, Pennsylvania area, Marissa Dobson now resides about an hour from Washington, D.C. She is a lady who likes to keep busy, and is always busy doing something. With two different college degrees, she believes you are never done learning.

Being the first daughter to an avid reader, this gave her the advantage of learning to read at a young age. Since learning to read she has always had her nose in a book. It wasn't until she was a teenager that she started writing down the stories she came up with.

Marissa is blessed with a wonderful supportive husband, Thomas. He is her other half and allows her to stay home and pursue her writing. He puts up with all her quirks and listens to her brainstorm in the middle of the night?

Her writing buddies Max (a cocker spaniel) and Dawne (a beagle mix) are always around to listen to me bounce ideas off them. They might not be able to answer, but they are helpful in their own ways.

She love to hear from readers so send her an email at marissa@marissadobson.com or visit her website www.marissadobson.com

CPSIA information can be obtained at www.ICGtesting.com
Printed in the USA
LVOW11s1957160614

390268LV00001B/360/P